RAPTURE AT MIDNIGHT

The
Cynn Cruor Bloodline Series
Book 1

ISOBELLE CATE

This is a work of fiction. Names, characters, places and incidents are either the product of the author's imagination or used fictitiously, and any resemblance to actual persons, living or dead, business establishments, events or locales is entirely coincidental.

Rapture at Midnight
All rights reserved.
Copyright 2013 © Isobelle Cate

Cover by JRA Stevens

ALL RIGHTS RESERVED. This book contains material protected under International and Federal Copyright Laws and Treaties. Any unauthorized reprint or use of this material is prohibited. No part of this book may be reproduced or transmitted in any form or by any means, electronic or mechanical, including photocopying, recording, or by any information storage and retrieval system without express written permission from the author / publisher.

She is the very essence of his immortal life.
He is her soul.

Finn Qualtrough, a Cynn Cruor warrior, is on a mission to find leader of the Scatha Cruor, Dac Valerian. When he pursues three Scatha warriors who can lead him to Dac, he discovers a woman who awakens a desire within Quinn to claim her as his own.

Eirene Spence is an insomniac and a computer genius. Her penchant for midnight walks in the park puts her life in danger when the Scatha Cruor find her. She is saved when a handsome stranger rescues her. His touch ignites a hunger inside her that only he can satisfy.

By a twist of fate, Eirene's client is Dac Valerian. She can lead Finn--and the rest of the Cynn Cruor--to Dac's lair. But now Dac wants her dead.

Now Finn must fulfill his mission while trying to keep Eirene alive. With Valarian after Eirene, nothing is certain, not even her place in Finn's life.

There is a-growing war between the Cynn Cruor and the Scatha Cruor: two breeds of immortal warriors who carry human, vampire, and werewolf blood. The Cynn Cruor wants to live in harmony with the human race. The Scatha Cruor wants to enslave them.

It's time to start preparing for battle.

Warning: intended for mature audiences 18+

Isobelle Cate

Acknowledgments

To everyone in Beau Coup, you have been such a great blessing and moving force in my writing career. You have given me a chance to be heard and taught me to be better.

Special thanks go to Emily A. Lawrence, Jennifer Stevens, and Dianne Dixon. Not only have you helped me make my stories come to fruition, but you've also enriched my life with your laughter, wisdom, and everything else in between. Thank you so much.

To the Cate's Renegades Street Team. You keep me going all the time. We shall go from strength to strength. Thank you for your support.

To my family. Thank you for the pizza, the coffee, the wine, your advice, laughter, patience, and insight even at 5 am. I love you both.

To all the authors I have had the good fortune to know in this incredible journey, thank you for allowing me to read and learn from you. To my betas, readers, new readers, bloggers, and to those who have been with me from the very start. My characters and I are truly humbled and honoured that you have allowed us to be a part of your lives.

I'm having such a fantastic adventure. Thank you.

Isobelle Cate

PROLOGUE

Pluscarden, Elgin, Scotland 1712

The branches whipped against their cloaks while moonlight streamed through the overhanging tree branches. The smell of the impending snowstorm was strong in the wind, as though it too was chasing them.

The rider ahead of the small group looked back to see if her companions were still following. Finn rode between his parents. At eleven years old he could hold his own, keeping a tight rein on the spirited Arabian thoroughbred. His heart thundered in tandem with his horse's frantic gallop. His face jerked from left to right to avoid being whipped by low hanging boughs, but he knew from the stings and moisture he felt on his face, that they had already drawn blood. The freezing cold would numb the scrapes and welts soon. It didn't matter. His wounds would heal by the time they reached their destination. After all, he was a Cynn Cruor.

Finn looked back. His father took the rear guard. He too glanced back from whence they came, making sure they weren't being followed. Finn faced front again. It was a good thing his mother had tied her brown tresses and placed them underneath the cowl of her cloak. At their breakneck speed, her hair could become entangled in the branches, whip her off her horse and snap her neck just like Absalom of the Bible.

Finn closed his eyes for a moment as he forced the morbid thought away. How could things have changed so drastically in a matter of hours? Earlier that evening they had been having a wonderful post-Christmas supper. He had gone up to his room in the manor as his mother bade him to get a good night's sleep. His head had barely touched the pillow when his father entered his room to rouse him from bed.

"It's time," his father had said, his mouth in a grim line.

Finn and his family had prepared for this day for as long as he could remember, it had become second nature to plan what to bring and what to leave behind. Now that the day had arrived, he experienced a momentary sense of panic. His mind closed and he didn't know what to do.

"*Qualtrough!*"

Finn's head snapped at his father's voice. His mother's worried eyes looked at him in a moment of compassion before that emotion disappeared and she nodded to him. Finn reddened with shame. His father strode to him and knelt down to his height. The understanding and sadness he saw in his father's gaze made his own eyes smart.

"*Dinnae feel bad that you lost yer heid for a moment, lad.*" *His father's mouth quirked into a slight smile.* "*It happens to all of us. Never for one moment feel you are not worthy of the Cynn Cruor name.*"

Finn swallowed.

"*Aye Da.*"

"*Let's go. Mam's waiting with the horses.*" *His father straightened and checked the bags Finn held.* "*We need to get to the abbey as soon as possible.*"

As though his memories had the ability to conjure it, the huge and shadowy facade of the abbey came into view buffeted against the black grey sky. Before their horses even reached the stone fence which separated the abbey from the outside world, its huge wooden gates were thrown open. Their horses sped through before several monks pushed the gates back and bolted them.

Finn climbed down from his stallion and numbly

gave the reins to one of the monks who stood waiting.

"Come Finn and warm yerself." His mother's soft voice was a balm to his fear, her breath puffing around her like a mystic veil. She fished out a cloth from underneath her cloak to gingerly wipe away the blood trickling down Finn's cheeks. He looked up at her. She was smiling, but behind the smile he saw something he didn't want to accept.

Anguish.

"Mam, is there anything wrong?"

His mother blinked. "Nay Finn. Come, yer father's with Abbot Hugh. We cannae keep them waiting."

Finn followed his mother inside. She wore a man's clothes underneath her woollen cloak. Both their soft soled leather boots made nary a sound on the cold stone floor of the abbey. Finn looked around the arched passageways which enclosed a courtyard with a statue of a saint in the centre. Except for the monks who had closed the gates behind them and those who took their horses, there was no one in sight.

"Finn!"

His head whipped back towards his mother who was already several feet away. He ran towards her. She immediately veered to the right to open a heavy wooden door. She entered and left Finn to close the door behind him.

The high vaulted room was illuminated with so many candles, if Finn didn't know any better; he would have thought it was mid-morning. Across the room, he saw his father and the abbot talking in whispers as they both looked at the weapons lying on the wooden table. His eyes widened. How could a holy place have so many instruments of death? His mother began taking sgian dubhs, sharp daggers which fit snugly into her boots and into the sheaths tied around her upper arms. His father took two evil looking broadswords and strapped them across his back. With his face filled with determination, Finn walked towards them and began gathering his own weapons. His parents would need all the help they could get. But before he could sheath his own sgian dubh at his waist, his father's hand stalled him.

"Nay, Finn," he said, his voice gruff. "You are staying with the abbot."

"Why?"

Suddenly Finn was angry as the tension of the past few hours crested over him.

"Why cannae I hae a weapon?" He looked back and forth at his parents. His mother's mouth was pinched. She wavered for a moment before she continued to collect her weapons. The queue that held his father's shoulder length hair fell to the stone floor when his father raked his hand through it. Finn picked up the leather tie and gave it to his sire. And there in his father's eyes, he saw the same anguish and something more.

Despair.

Finn stood bewildered. His knees threatened to buckle beneath him. He knew what they were going to do.

"You are not leaving me," he said, channelling his pain and fury into his voice. He shook his head as his chest tightened at the inevitability of it all.

He saw his father swallow hard before he turned to look at his mother, whose tears streamed down her face. He ran to her and was immediately enveloped in her desperate, but warm embrace. The numerous weapons sheathed in her body pressed hard against him, yet Finn didn't care. He didn't want his parents to leave. He had to think of something. He had to find a way to keep them all together. But, what? He gritted his teeth so he wouldn't cry, but his tears were as stubborn as he was. Despite his resolve, they traced their sad pathway down his cheeks. He turned his head slightly when his peripheral vision noticed his father's approach. Finn reached out to also embrace his sire.

"Please, let me go with you." Finn's voice was muffled against his father's chest while he kept a tight hold of his shirt and his mother's vest, as if by doing so, they would all be fused together.

"You are not yet of age, Finn." His father's voice was tight. "This is a very difficult decision for us to leave you. But it's because we love you that we have to do so."

"I am a Cynn Cruor," Finn stressed. "If we fight, we heal quickly."

"Nay," it was his mother who spoke now. "The children of the Cynn Cruor remain vulnerable until they become grown men and find their mate."

"If I die, then I die. I willna let you leave me."

"Finn you are the last of our line," his father said. "We will come back for you when the time comes. You have to be kept safe. Abbot Hugh is a Cynn mortal and your uncle."

Finn looked at the abbot without seeing and he didn't care if he was his uncle. What mattered more was that life as he knew it was unravelling. Then belatedly, he gave the abbot his attention.

The abbot's face was thinner and weathered. But he had the same eyes as his father's and there was a huge amount of kindness and compassion in them at the moment.

"I beg your leave sir, and pardon my manners, but I cannae stay with you."

"That's enough, Master Qualtrough." His father's voice was quiet, but to Finn it sounded like the crack of thunder.

Finn stepped back as though his father had slapped him. He saw the pain and remorse in his father's eyes. After a few moments his father held out his hand. Reluctantly, Finn took it and they both walked towards the wooden bench by the wall and sat down. The howling wind sounded as though hundreds of ghosts surrounded them. The windows rattled in their lead fittings. The wind which seeped through the cracks in the stone walls made the candles flicker. But nothing frightened Finn as much as the fear of losing his parents.

He waited for his father to speak.

"So young, with a man's task ahead of you," his father murmured heavily under his breath. He shook himself out of his musings to face his son. His mouth curved to half a sad smile. "You have to let us go, Finn. The Cynn Cruors hae been called together and we hae to heed the call. You are not the only Cynn child being left by his parents."

"But you told me that whenever a war breaks out the mother stays."

His father looked at Finn's mother.

"Aye," his father conceded. "But it's the Cynn Eald who has called us to arms."

"Is that supposed to make me feel better?" Finn asked bitterly. He swiped the tears from his cheeks, unmindful of the sting it caused against the scratches on his face.

His father shook his head.

"No, but to a Cynn Cruor warrior sometimes duty is bigger than family. The war has to stop so we can live peacefully with humans. And if this is our chance to stop the conflict, then we must do all we can."

Finn's shoulders slumped.

"We will come back, Finn." His father chucked his

chin gently.

"Promise?"

"We will do our best."

It was the least Finn could hope for. He nodded automatically in resignation.

Abbot Hugh led them back to the abbey's entrance door. After embracing his brother, Finn's father turned to him. Finn extended his hand, but his father took him into his arms and embraced him with all the love he had for his son. Finn's throat thickened with emotion, yet he refused to cry any more. Next, it was his mother's turn. As she held him close, he breathed in her familiar scent. The scent of dawn and early morning dew, the scent of comfort and undying love.

"Be brave, my darling Finn." His mother planted kisses all over his face as she tried to stem the flow of her tears. She held him tight against her body and breathed him in, as though she was trying to keep a memento of her son to bring with her. "We will see you soon."

"I will be brave, Mam," he said as he embraced her tightly. "And ye both be careful and come back to me."

And then they were gone. Abbot Hugh kept him in a gentle hold as the doors closed behind his parents and the night swallowed them.

As the gates closed behind his parents, so did the gates lock around his heart. Finn wished he could cry out the anguish and desolation which lay claim to him, but no further tears dropped from his eyes, even though deep in his heart he knew he would never see his parents again.

CHAPTER ONE

Manchester, United Kingdom, Present Day

"This doesn't make any bloody sense!" Eirene muttered underneath her breath. She had spent hours trying to understand the strange source code. She swore she'd never seen anything like it before. At first she'd hardly noticed it, as everything looked sequential, but when she started to create the code which would make her client's system more secure, it refused to work. That was when Eirene noticed the source code was not just something which made the client's system run.

The strange code used very ancient symbols; symbols that Eirene knew were thousands of years old. How or why such symbols were imbedded into a computer language baffled and excited her. This was something hardly anyone else would notice. Only someone like her, who had an interest in semiotics, would pick up on this oddity. Her adoptive father, a closet scholar, loved to share his discoveries about symbols which he saw everywhere. At first Eirene thought he had gone a little off his rocker, but the more she was exposed to his ramblings, the more she understood and became aware of the different symbols all around her.

She saw so many symbols, she was beginning to believe she too, had gone daft.

However, as she watched the number codes scrolling up her monitor, she couldn't deny what she saw. A symbol embedded in the computer's code which looked like writhing snakes forming the letters 'S'and 'C'. She had no bloody idea what it meant except it was making it damn difficult for her to create the source code needed to keep the system fail-safe and protected.

Eirene leaned back in her ergonomic chair, utterly frustrated and disgusted with herself. No, correction. Disgusted with the symbols. She needed to make the code work. She and Devon needed more funds for their charity and with the economic downturn plaguing the UK, they needed to shore up their capital so they could keep on working while living on the interest from their savings.

Working on finding Devon's daughter, Penny.

Eirene used her computer prowess to infiltrate computer systems in the hope she might find clues to Penny's whereabouts. First, she hacked the Manchester International Airport's CCTV system and found two clips of footage of Penny and Janice, Devon's wife. The second bit of footage showed mother and daughter enter a Volvo SUV which vanished into the night. Since then, she'd infiltrated the computer systems of other UK airports and several possibly unscrupulous organizations, hoping she could find some lead to Penny's whereabouts. But nada.

Now this system she'd been working on for some time had ancient symbols embedded into the original code. It looked promising. She worried her lower lip as she looked at the information in front of her. Why would someone make it difficult to fix the code? Unless they were hiding something and to repair it could open a can of worms?

She reached out for her mobile phone to check the time. Midnight. She sighed as she moved her head from left to right to roll the tension off her neck. Though her mind felt as if a wooly mammoth had decided to take up residence in it, she was still wide awake. An insomniac, that was what she was, she thought glumly. She wanted to call Devon, but the poor man was probably more than half way into dreamland by now.

Eirene stood up and walked across the room, placing her mug on the tray which sat on top of the personal fridge. With one last look at the computer and CCTV monitors, she let herself out of her attic office. She went down one flight of stairs to get her telescopic baton and black zipped hoodie, shrugging into it as she made her way to the ground floor. On her way out of her house, she switched on the alarm and closed her front door before double locking it.

The balmy night soothed her frayed nerves. She inhaled deeply, allowing the fresh air to wake her sluggish veins. She looked up at the sky. The waxing moon gently lit her way. She raised the hood of her sweatshirt to hide her long blue black hair and her face. It was already stupid of her to walk alone at midnight. No point in advertising the fact she was female.

The streetlights cast shadows everywhere, but Eirene wasn't afraid. There was something about the dark which beckoned to her and soothed her soul. It didn't frighten her. It was as if the night knew she felt at home in it and welcomed her without question.

Headlights of a car bounced against the road. Quickly, Eirene moved to the shadows until the blazing white Benz with speakers blaring out the latest Bollywood song whizzed by. Eirene left the shadows and continued towards the Whitmore Road gate of Platt Field's Park. Her ballet flats made nary a sound on the pavement until she reached the dirt path leading to the park's manmade lake where her feet crunched over the small stones. She cringed. She needed to practice walking more silently. She stepped over the packed earth and into the grass. Satisfied that she could feel the soft ground underneath her feet, she continued walking towards the hill which faced the south side of the lagoon.

She had just crossed the opposite end of the lake, close to the tennis courts, when she heard growls and screeches which sent her heart plummeting to her feet. She whirled towards the direction of the sound. The noise was coming from the copse of trees that provided a natural barrier between the open park and the lake. Eirene controlled her breathing even as a trickle of fear danced its way down her spine. She was almost out in the open. She just hoped whatever was making that sound couldn't see her.

But she would be able to see them. Far as long as she could remember, her eyesight had always been much better at night. She not only saw shadows, but was also able to partly make out a person's features. This night-vision proved to be a gift she was grateful for, especially when she went out at night and couldn't risk letting the scum of the earth know she was female.

Quickly, she changed direction and ran to the birch tree about four feet away from her. Before she could reach it, she stifled a scream. Three forms jumped high into the air, landing a few feet away, surrounding her. Eirene whipped her telescopic baton from her pocket and flicked it to expand it to full length. She'd be able to dodge them.

"Looks like we're going to have fun tonight," one of the men laughed. "Male or female, it doesn't matter to us."

"Asshole!" Eirene gave one of them a back handed whip with her baton. A small amount of satisfaction lit her face when she heard bones crack. She retreated a little and resumed her defensive stance.

Nothing prepared her for what she saw.

Their eyes suddenly glowed a dark green.

"How the hell can dark green glow?" Eirene muttered underneath her breath, staring at them in disbelief. The green she saw wasn't even the neon kind of green. Neither did their eyes look like the light coming from night vision goggles worn inverted. Their eyes were just that.

A glowing dark green.

That wasn't all. Her eyes widened as she took several steps back. The faces of the three men in front of her morphed with big jowls filled with razor sharp teeth. The stench of the saliva dripping from their mouths reminded Eirene of rotting garbage left to decompose where it lay. She tried to suck in her breath, but almost gagged. As the appearance of the three men changed, a new smell assaulted her nostrils. The smell of someone who hadn't bathed in ages. That did it. Fear she could handle. Stench? She drew the line with that one.

She sensed the movement from the creature at her left and before the three knew what was happening, Eirene swiftly turned around to give each of them a round house kick. One of the creatures quickly recovered and made a grab for her. She deftly leaned to her right side while bringing her baton down hard on his arm. He screamed. Eirene didn't stop to admire her handiwork. She sprinted away from them making her way to the Shakespearean Gardens. There was a place she used inside the grove when she wanted to stay out without being seen. No way would she return to her house. With those human animals chasing her, returning to the house would spell death.

The howls of fury continued behind her, but didn't sound as though the brutes were in pursuit. Eirene continued to push herself to the point of her lungs almost bursting with exertion. At last she saw the grove's gate. She vaulted over the fence and tumbled down the slope. Wincing as some of the bramble bushes stung her hands, she stood up and crammed herself into her hideaway. She took huge gasps of air and tried as hard as possible not to make any noise at all. Her lungs clawed against her ribcage as she tried to breathe without making a sound, but she couldn't, and her vision swam slightly. With her knees hugged to her chest and her stomach squeezed against her spine, Eirene couldn't take in as much air as she needed. Risking a little noise to move to a less uncomfortable position, she sighed, but soon heard the screeching by the garden's gate.

Their stares moved eerily in the dark. Eirene could see their eyes clearly as the creatures turned their heads from left to right. She found it difficult to swallow with the lump of fear clogging her throat, her heart knocking about inside her ribcage.

The glowing dark green orbs locked to where she sat hidden. Their screeching changed to yaps of evil delight. Eirene felt a wave of helplessness squeeze her gut like a vise. If only she had listened to Devon. He had told her not to go out at night, but being cooped up inside her house drove her mad.

There was no point in belabouring the issue now. She was in this bind, and as the creatures moved closer to her hiding place, she braced herself. No way in hell were they going to take her alive.

If she could, she'd take all of them down with her.

Suddenly, a hand clamped over her mouth and stifled her scream.

CHAPTER TWO

Finn swore softly when he felt teeth bite hard into his palm. He encircled the female's waist with his other arm, bringing her back flush against his chest and her butt against his groin. The wave of lust which hit him came out of nowhere. He hissed as he felt his cock coming to life, the pain of her bite only increasing his arousal.

"If you don't want to be mauled by those men out there you will keep still," he spoke harshly into her ear. It wasn't only because the Scatha Cruor were closing in on them. If the body in front of him didn't stop moving, his thick arousal might demand that he bury himself within her. He had never been in a situation where he had to battle the Scatha while keeping a tight rein on his response to a female's delectable body. He clenched his jaw in an effort to stop the urge to cup the underside of her right breast. Ancients! How could he think of sex at a time like this?

Finn felt her heartbeat thud against his forearm like a hummingbird. She stopped moving, but remained tense. He felt her teeth unlatch from his palm. Finn relaxed somewhat, then growled softly when he felt the tip of her tongue swipe his hand. His rod immediately twitched in attention.

"We don't have much time." Finn whispered, unmindful of his interested manhood. "If I take my hand away will you scream?"

It took a heartbeat before she shook her head jerkily, even though her body continued to tremble.

The growls closed in on them. This time the female moulded herself to him as though she wanted to hide inside his skin. Finn inhaled sharply before he closed his eyes and concentrated on throwing their scent off. Finn heard the Scatha stop in their tracks. They swore in frustration. He smiled, even though using his gift had partly drained him. He opened his eyes to see the Scatha run in the opposite direction from where he and the female hid.

Finn relaxed and reluctantly let go of the girl in front of him. As soon as he did, she jumped away to turn and face him.

He felt as if someone had just punched him in the gut.

With his superior Cynn Cruor eyesight he could see her as though it were daylight. His gaze zeroed in on her mouth, slightly parted as she took huge gulps of air. Her lips looked like a dusky pink cupid's bow in the moonlight. Finn could only guess how blush red they looked during the day. He wanted to taste them and feel them against his own lips, to taste her as he sweetly invaded her mouth. Her face was framed by high cheekbones, the same dusky pink color of her lips. Her pert nose lightly flared as she inhaled deeply and quickly. And her eyes. Ancients! He wouldn't mind drowning in those sable coloured pools surrounded by thick lashes. And though she was covered in black, the way her jeans hugged her legs allowed Finn to imagine how the rest of her body looked. Firm, but shapely.

And definitely sexy. He also knew the female was mortal.

Except for the Deoré, the Ancient Cynn's beloved, there was no female Cynn Cruor.

Finn had an overwhelming urge to protect her and it stopped him cold. He rapidly blinked his eyes. Where had that idea come from? He shook off the thought. If there was any feeling of protection, it was because the female would no doubt have been mauled by the Scatha Cruors. He had seen her take on all three of the Scatha, fighting like a she-cat. This female might be mortal, but she was certainly not ordinary.

Protecting and caring for someone else for a long period of time was not part of Finn's agenda. It wasn't part of his life. While he was attracted to this female, he had no time for others who didn't have the same goal he and his Cynn Cruor brethren shared. To put an end to the Scatha Cruors. He didn't want the added burden which came with the feeling of responsibility he had for the girl who stood before him. He felt the need to protect her, and he fought against the inclination with everything he had in him. He also couldn't understand how he could feel this way towards someone he'd just barely met. He scowled as he looked up to the sky, seeing the shape of the waxing moon. Now, it made sense. He let his body relax. His strange behaviour could probably be explained by the fact that it was seven more nights until the full moon and his wereblood was beginning to kick in. That was why he was feeling something towards the female, he reasoned. He and the rest of the Cynn Cruors assigned to Manchester would need to find a way to expend their lust. His thoughts returned to the girl, no, *woman,* who faced him. His eyes narrowed as he swore inwardly. He would be no different from the Scatha if he used her to slake his need. He was here to kill the Scatha responsible for the death of his parents. That was his only mission. Damn the need to find a mate.

The baton held firmly in her right hand pointed at the ground, but Finn knew she would use it on him if he made a wrong move. He couldn't believe his eyes earlier when he saw her take down three Scatha, catching them unawares. No mortal had ever survived a Scatha attack, and Finn had to grudgingly admit some admiration for her spunk.

"Who are you?"

"I'm not going to hurt you," he said as he stood up quickly. His movement made the female move back two steps, her baton above her head.

"That's not what I asked," she said as her gaze narrowed.

"Who I am is irrelevant."

"Irrelevant to what?"

"Sorry?"

"Irrelevant to what?" She repeated. "Those men...no, creatures came after me and were close to finding out where we were, and then suddenly they turned away. And as much as I don't want to admit it, you saved my life. So again, who are you? How do I know you're not one of them?"

"I will never be one of them." Finn snapped, his anger at the Scatha quickly filling him. Turning away from her, he swore, angry at himself. He ran his hands through his hair. Damn! She was right. She didn't know him and he could be one of them. If she decided to use her baton on him, he wouldn't blame her. Finn wasn't exactly acting as though she could trust him. For days he'd been tracking the three Scatha, and he couldn't believe his luck when he found them in Platt Fields. He would have killed them already if the female hadn't showed up.

"I'm not angry at you," he spoke quietly, turning his head slightly over his shoulder. "I've been after those three for some time now." Why he was telling her his reason was beyond him, but it seemed right to do so. As if it was the most natural thing in the world to do.

"What were they?"

Before Finn could answer, ear piercing screeches rent the air. He grabbed the female and shoved her behind him. He had no time to whip out his knife as two of the Scatha barrelled into him. With a roar he pushed them away from him, his vampire and werewolf blood taking over. He could feel his eyes changing and knew they were going to be blood orange. With deftness and precision, he grabbed the claws of one Scatha and used it to sever the other one's head. Immediately, the beheaded Scatha turned to dust. Finn next turned to the second, sending a right hook across its face, which made it fly a few feet from him. As Finn ran, he whipped out his knife with a silver double serrated edge and plunged it into its black heart before taking it out to sever the head from the body in less than a second.

Adrenalin pumping in his veins and breathing heavily, Finn turned to the last surviving enemy. His eyes narrowed as he saw the female skilfully parry the Scatha's blows while she was able to hit him several times with her baton. Hoping she wouldn't see how his eyes changed colour, he ran towards them, and as he did, the female ducked to avoid the swipe of the sharp claws. They raked across Finn's chest instead. It wasn't deep, but blinding pain hit him as he felt his blood seep and drip down his shirt. His ability to cloak their scent had sapped a lot of his energy. With his remaining strength, Finn gripped the handle of his knife and sliced through the Scatha's neck. The creature fell to the ground, but didn't turn to dust. Finn fell down on his knees. He could feel himself weaken. He felt the female's soft hand wrench the knife from his grasp as his eyes became heavy. In an instant dust billowed around him.

* * * *

"I have to get you to a hospital." Eirene knelt in front of her saviour. She dropped both the baton and the knife before she unzipped her hoodie and placed it on his wounds to stem the flow of blood.

Eirene fished her mobile phone from out of her

jean's right pocket, when a strong hand gripped her wrist.

"No hospital," he said, gritting his teeth. "My phone. In my pocket. Get it."

Eirene didn't hesitate. The man was bleeding for Chrissakes! As she reached into his pocket, heat flared through her hand and her cheeks, her fingers feeling the strong sinew of his thigh muscle as she searched for the phone. Eirene's breath hitched when she heard him groan. She swallowed hard. There! Her hand closed around the phone and fished it out before she tarried any longer.

Eirene handed him the cell. He pressed the call button.

"Where are you?" The voice from the speaker phone asked tersely.

"Need extraction, Roarke," he replied. "All Scatha killed."

"Where the hell are you, Finn?"

"Your wounds need to be cleaned up." Eirene interrupted him. She lifted the sweatshirt from his chest and winced. "You really need to get to the hospital."

"Who is with you, Qualtrough?"

Eirene heard the concern in the voice, but also a hint of quiet anger.

The man called Finn Qualtrough sighed tiredly before his arm fell to the ground.

"Finn! You bloody well better answer me!"

That's it! Her own anger about to boil over, Eirene grabbed the mobile phone from Finn's hand.

"Listen asshole or whoever you are. Your man here needs medical attention. He's got four gashes on his chest and he's losing blood," she snapped. "Now either you shut the hell up, save the interrogation for later and come get him, or I call an ambulance and get him to the hospital myself." Finn's arm lifted to try to get the mobile phone from her, but she scowled at him and swatted his hand as if it was a pesky fly.

There was silence on the other end of the phone.

"Okay, I'm calling an ambulance." Eirene took out her own mobile phone to dial 999.

"Where are you?" The voice asked. This time there was no anger, but there was a tinge of worry.

"I'm taking him to my house. He can't be left here out in the open," Eirene replied.

"Understood."

She gave her address and ended the call. Eirene placed both phones in one pocket and her baton in the other. When she looked at the knife there was no blood.

Damn! What had she gotten herself into? And why was she so calm? Why wasn't she freaking out after seeing beings that would have put Jason or Freddie Kruger to shame? Now that the creatures were dead, her initial fear had dissipated. In its place was a curious and grudging attraction towards the man lying on the ground. The stranger, who had arrived just in time to save her, exuded a dangerous appeal which called to her. For some unknown reason she felt safe with him. Which didn't make sense. This man could turn out to be like those they had just killed. Why did this ruggedly handsome stranger have to be the first man to appeal to her in ages?

There was no time to mull over the consequences of her actions. She looked down at the one she now knew as Finn Qualtrough. He appeared to have lost consciousness. Eirene heaved a long sigh.

"Finn," she said, nudging his shoulder gently. He didn't answer. She shook him a little harder this time. He moved his head and opened his eyes.

Eirene's heart went out to him. There was so much

pain in those eyes.

"I'll get you home. You'll be extracted from there," she said, using his term.

He nodded, sitting up slowly.

"Don't! You're bleeding." Eirene held him up but when her sweatshirt fell from his chest, she gasped.

The blood had stopped. The gashes were no longer open. By the light of the moon she could tell there were still dark streaks on his skin, but now the wounds looked like they were about to scab over.

"What the hell are you?" She breathed.

"Help me up," Finn said, not bothering to answer her.

Eirene placed his arm around her shoulders and assisted him to stand up. All the while she was very conscious of the heat that emanated from his body, drugging her into a sense of security. She reckoned he was about six feet tall, for the top of her head only reached Finn's shoulder. The warmth of his body by her side was the most delicious thing she had ever experienced. When he placed his arm around her neck, she almost couldn't stop the sigh that wanted to come tumbling from her lips. His skin scorched the flesh left bare by her tank top. She sucked in her breath when Finn's hand brushed the top of her right breast, his fingers almost coming down to rest on her covered nipple.

"Am I too heavy?" His breath fanned the hair on the top of her head. The timbre of his voice was soft, but deep, and it brought an aching awareness to her body. He smelled of pine, spice, and rugged maleness. Fresh, hot, and all man. How could a stranger whom she should be afraid of awaken her body in the most sensual way? All her senses were attuned to his every move, to the sound of his voice. How could this be? Heat coursed through her with every breath he took.

"No," her voice was hoarse. "You're not that heavy."

He gave a small chuckle before he eased off a little of his weight Eirene carried. He groaned when Eirene encircled his waist.

"Did I hurt you?" She looked up, suddenly worried that he might have sustained more injuries than she was aware of. When her gaze met his, she almost gasped at the desire she saw in his eyes. He had the most beautiful eyes. They were black with gold flecks, or were they dark blue? His hunger rocked her body, sending delicious tingles down to her sex. She saw his gaze fall to her mouth. Her heart, which was already hammering in her chest, notched up a level. He looked like he was going to kiss her. She should be appalled.

But God! She wanted to feel his mouth on hers. She wanted to know how his tongue felt mating with hers. How it felt on her skin and all over her body.

Then Finn bent down. His breath brushed the tendrils of her hair by her neck. Eirene held her breath, her lids at half-mast. She gasped and closed her eyes when she felt his tongue swirl over the pulse at the base of her throat. Then his lips skimmed the sensitive skin on the side of her neck and up to her earlobe. She couldn't stop the sighs which escaped her lips when his tongue blazed a trail over the shell of her ear. He lightly nibbled on her earlobe before his lips moved to the corner of her mouth.

This was wrong, Eirene's mind screamed, but her body argued for her to get a little taste, for this chance might not come again. She nearly melted against Finn. She was a puppet in his arms and her strings were deliberately entangling themselves around him. In surrender, Eirene turned towards him, her palm resting on his chest, over his heart. She could feel it hammering hard beneath her hand. He appeared to be as affected as she was. She angled her mouth so that his lips brushed hers. Their mixed breaths made their arousal more palpable.

"No, you didn't hurt me." Finn's deep voice made her feel like melting chipotle chocolate.

Sweet and hot.

"We have to get you to the house, Finn." Eirene said, surprised at how easily she said his name and how normal her voice was. "You're injured."

"What we're doing is going to help me heal." Finn rubbed his lips along her forehead, like he was marking her. The sensual movement allowed his chin to graze against her mouth. Eirene closed her eyes, enjoying the sensation and couldn't resist nipping at his chin. Finn growled softly in response, and pulled her close, flush against him.

"How?" Eirene moaned with pleasure when her palms moved down his taut abdomen, carefully avoiding the part where the gashes were still fresh. Liquid heat pooled between her legs when she felt his huge arousal nudging her thigh. Her heart was speeding like a bullet train. Instead of answering her, Finn brought his mouth to hers. He kissed her tentatively, giving her a chance to back out. When she didn't, he nipped at her lips. Eirene sighed as she returned the kiss, letting the tip of her tongue trail over the seam of his mouth. With a groan, Finn claimed her lips. His tongue pressed through the barrier of her teeth and into her mouth, making Eirene gasp with pleasure. Red hot lava suffused her veins. Her pulse beat faster and harder. Her sex involuntarily clenched as her stomach muscles contracted. She held on to Finn for dear life when his hand curved around the base of her head, and slanted his mouth against hers to further deepen the kiss.

Eirene didn't know which was up or down as their tongues mated, swirling around each other, getting acquainted with one another. Somewhere deep in her mind, she knew instinctively that her mouth was made for his. She didn't know how she knew this, just that it felt so right. She moaned softly when Finn's hand came between them to cup her breast. She broke the kiss to arch her back and give herself up to his touch. Eyes closed and holding on to his biceps, she whimpered her approval when he pulled her tank and bra down far enough to free her breast. When his warm mouth closed over her nipple and suckled hard, she cried out, lust swirling around and taking her towards an impending storm. A fresh wave of heat soaked her panties as Finn continued to lave and kiss one aroused nipple before moving to the other, while his fingers tweaked the one his mouth had just left. She would have come right there, had Finn not abruptly broken the kiss to step a little away from her. Suddenly feeling rudderless, Eirene almost stumbled as the balmy air felt like an arctic wind after Finn's body heat, her nipples now hardened by the night's gentle breeze.

"This has to stop. We have to go." Finn said brusquely.

His statement was like a splash of cold water and for a while she floundered, trying to get her bearings. What had just happened? Eirene willed her heart to calm down, but her pulse still thudded erratically. Humiliation heated her face. She kept her head down while she righted her front, her breasts still tingling from Finn's wicked mouth. She couldn't be as abrupt as Finn. She wasn't sure what she'd expected him to say, but it wasn't this. Her past came at her like a runaway train, the memories running through her mind like the blurred scenery outside a train's window. Finn had seduced her. For what? She had fallen for his spiel, implying the kiss would heal him. She did see evidence of that, but. She stopped her thoughts abruptly. She wouldn't even dare to delve that deep.

Story of my life. Idiotically thinking I mean something to someone.

Finn had seduced her and she had allowed herself to be seduced. It was her fault as much as his, but she'd die before admitting it. End of story.

Why was she such a sucker for bad boys?

It only took another minute to clear her mind.

"No," she said flatly. "You don't have to go anywhere." She took out his mobile phone from her pocket and pressed the last number dialled. It was immediately answered.

"We're on our way," the voice said.

"No need to go to my address. Your Finn Qualtrough has healed himself." Eirene said, her anger barely suppressed, giving Finn a withering stare. "And if I so much as see any car or anyone who looks like this jerk anywhere near my house, I will call the police." She ended the call and hurled the mobile phone at Finn, which he caught in mid-air. She bent down to get her baton and pointedly looked at Finn's dagger on the ground. She knew Finn watched her and she hated her body for reacting to his stare, disgusted with the excitement trickling down her spine. She shouldn't care. All she wanted was to get home before her angry tears fell. She started walking.

"Where are you going?" Finn's voice stopped her. It was not much of a question.

Eirene turned around to glare at him.

"What does it look like? I'm going home. Since it appears your wounds have healed and you're standing on

31

your own, you don't need me. You got your kicks."

"That's not what this was about." Finn snapped as he raked his hand through his hair, wincing when his healing skin stretched.

"Oh, right." Eirene's voice dripped with sarcasm. "It was payment for saving me."

"I said, enough!"

Eirene arched an eyebrow. "Who gave you the right to command me?"

She saw him flinch, but kept silent. She held her baton in a death grip as though it was a lifeline against insanity. Finn continued to watch her with narrowed eyes. Her body was shaking with self-loathing, but her eyes conveyed the fury inside her when she looked at him. Silence reigned between them, the wind so silent as if to see what would happen next.

"If you follow me, your injuries will be more grievous than mere scratches. What those damned fiends did to you will look like child's play. I promise you." Her voice was deadly soft.

Slowly, Eirene backed up. As soon as she reached the slope of the grove, she turned around and immediately vaulted over the stone wall and ran away as fast as she could from a memory she hoped to erase.

CHAPTER THREE

Bloody hell! If his Cynn brothers were with him at that very moment, Finn would have asked one of them to punch him in the face. He had royally fucked up the whole situation. He shouldn't have kissed her. He was no different from the Scatha he hunted. He had seen the disdain in her eyes and felt disgusted with himself, but he'd needed her kiss like he needed a shot of adrenalin. Using his gift of invisibility, cloaking their scent and being slashed by the Scatha had robbed him of much of his strength.

You could have waited for Zac to give you a shot of adriserum. Admit it...you kissed her because you wanted her. Healing be damned.

For the first time, he cursed the wereblood running through his veins. The werewolf DNA hiked their libido to a whole new level, especially in the few nights before the full moon. As soon as any young Cynn Cruor began their training, they were always taught to control their sexual urges, to keep a tight rein on the incredible sexual heat fuelled by their blood. Finn had never once given in to the urge to rut and had prided himself at his restraint even when he was out and about on the night of the full moon. He only had sex with women who came to him willingly. Both knew it was just the mating call. Nothing more. He had a mission, so nothing and no one was going to derail him from getting it done. On the other hand, the Scatha never cared about who their sex partners were as long as they could slake their lust. It didn't matter if the mortal was a child, adult, or even someone who already had one foot in the grave. Male or female, the Scatha had no preference when they defiled humans. They were indiscriminate rapists and debauched fiends.

This mortal, this female he'd just held in his arms had been different. His desire for her didn't stem from the need to be healed or an opportunity to slake his lust. He wanted more, beyond the hunger which drew him to her. He wanted to keep on kissing her and feel her nipples inside his mouth, to hear her cries of pleasure which had brought him such immense satisfaction, making him ramrod hard. This female's blood called to him. Her kisses had not only sent erotic images flashing through his mind, but they'd also started to penetrate the high wall around his heart, something that had not happened in close to three hundred years. As soon as his body had come into contact with hers, the stirrings he'd buried deep in his psyche began to awaken. He couldn't let that happen. He would never let that happen. He refused to care for someone else who could be taken from him. He had lost too much already.

Finn stared at his dagger on the ground and knelt down to pick it up. He had hurt her. When he'd moved away from her and told her what they had to do, he didn't need to use his Cynn Cruor gift to read her thoughts. Her pain and shame rippled across his mind like a stone thrown into a mirror smooth pond. And when he'd tasted her mouth. Ancients! Finn closed his eyes. Even now his cock twitched and demanded release inside the female's sweet sex, her nether lips lovingly and greedily sucking him inside her until he came. He imagined her channel continuing to milk him until he had nothing left.

Yes. He had messed this one up big time.

His mobile phone buzzed.

"Shakespearean Gardens in the park," was all he said before he disconnected the call. A sudden gust of wind ruffled his short hair.

The rest of the Cynn Cruor had arrived.

A low whistle came from over his right shoulder.

"No wonder you got hit. You took on the three Scatha all by yerself. Impressive."

Finn turned to look at Blake Strachan, the youngest Cynn Cruor in their team. He looked down at his torn shirt. Only then did he realize the female's hooded sweatshirt was on the ground. Remorse sluiced through him. He rubbed his chest to relieve the dull ache which developed. What the hell was happening to him? Why did this female affect him so much? It was just a kiss, for Ancients' sake!

"I killed two. A female mortal finished the other."

"Damn! Seriously?" Blake asked, his shock evident on his face. He whistled and looked around. "Where is she? I should congratulate her. Wow, eviscerating a Scatha. She must be one hell of a female."

A low growl rumbled out of Finn's chest, causing Blake's eyes to widen with surprise.

"Easy Finn." Blake grumbled. "What the hell's wrong with you?"

Yes, what the hell was wrong with him? Why didn't he like Blake asking about the female? Blake was like a younger brother to him. Finn had been his mentor. To snap at Blake because he admired the female he kissed was irrational. And if Blake did find her attractive enough to bed her, who was he to prevent his friend from taking the female?

Finn ran his hand through his hair in frustration. Part of him was glad she'd left. He didn't want them to know what she looked like. He wanted to be the only one to know her face, to know the softness of her lips and her body. However, the female didn't belong to him, so he shouldn't be bothered about his Cynn brethren asking about her. He had an illogical desire to protect her and claim her as his own. His stomach tightened at the thought of another man touching her. Bloody hell!

"Sorry Blake. That was uncalled for."

"You're damn right it was."

"Strachan, help Temple destroy whatever is left of the Scatha."

"No problem, Roarke." Blake said curtly and pivoted on his heel.

"Blake," Finn started.

Blake turned back to look at him before his mouth slowly lifted in a lopsided grin.

"It's okay, Bro." Blake said. "We're cool." He strode to Graeme Temple, who was inspecting what was left of the Scatha.

"Finn." Zac McBain greeted him. "Let's check your wounds, shall we?"

Finn nodded. He lifted his shirt to allow Zac to see how he was healing and saw Zac's brows rise.

"Don't."

Zac's lips pressed together in a thin line. He nodded before he strode to Blake and Graeme.

Finn turned to his left to glance at their leader, Roarke Hamilton. Roarke was as tall as Finn with the same short haircut, but where Finn's hair was all black, Roarke's was both black with greying hair at the temples. Like Finn, he looked like he was in his early thirties, even though he was three centuries older than Finn. His silver blue eyes surveyed the entire area of Shakespearean Gardens, not missing a thing.

Roarke's family had taken Finn in two centuries ago when his uncle, a Cynn mortal and monk had passed away. Roarke was like an older brother to him and his parents had showered Finn with all the love he could possibly ask for. While Finn was grateful and happy being part of the Hamilton family, nothing could remove the gaping hole in his heart that losing his parents had made.

"You okay?" Roarke looked at his second-in-command.

Finn nodded.

"Where is she?"

"It's not necessary, Roarke. She won't bother us." Finn replied, his jaw clenching.

Roarke whistled his breath out. "You know I can't allow that."

Finn swore underneath his breath before he heaved a sigh. Roarke was right. They needed to erase her memory about the existence of the Cruors. For both their sakes. It was how the Cynn had survived this long. It was also how mortals continued on with their lives, not knowing the depths of evil existing in the world. A Cynn Cruor warrior could never reveal their secrets to a human unless they claimed one as their chosen mate. Until then their two worlds had to remain separate. Erasing the female's memory was also the only way to help her remove the self-loathing she had for what they'd shared. She would not remember him. She would not remember the kiss. Finn felt as if a stone lay heavily in his gut.

"I'll do it."

Roarke arched a thick eyebrow, his arms crossed over his muscled chest.

"You sure about that? You're still healing, Finn. Your strength is not at an optimum level," he said. "It doesn't take a genius to see that something happened between the two of you, or you wouldn't be partially healed."

"I'm coming with you." Finn said as he faced Roarke. Irritation swept over Roarke's face. Finn didn't care. He wanted to be there when Roarke erased her memory.

Roarke stared at Graeme, Blake, and Zac several feet away from them. They were picking up the Scatha's clothes to dispose of them in a safe place.

"Does she mean that much to you?" Roarke asked, looking at him with curiosity.

The question was unexpected and it startled Finn. His eyes narrowed before turning to look at his Cynn Cruor brethren as well.

"It will pass."

For once Finn became uncomfortable under Roarke's cynosure, but eventually his team leader's shoulders appeared to relax. He nodded.

"Let's hope so. For your sake." He spared Finn a glance before ordering the rest of the Cynn to head back to the Faesten.

* * * *

Eirene woke with a groan. What was that infernal noise? Even in her groggy state, she knew it wasn't an alarm clock. Damn, it was her phone. She groped for it and groaned further when she saw the time. A heartbeat later, the name of the charity where she volunteered showed clearly on the mobile phone. She apologized to the person calling and told them she would be at the office in half an hour.

Under the warm shower's spray, Eirene pondered at what was happening to her. Insomnia always drove her to stay up until the early hours of the morning and she'd still have enough energy to continue during the day. Something had changed in the last couple of days. She was too dead tired to go to her attic office to work on her clients' programs and she hadn't had the chance to check on any CCTV footage. She hadn't even been to the park at midnight which was very unusual for her. She should be relieved that her insomnia seemed to have disappeared, but something in her subconscious nagged her. There was something more. If only she could remember.

"Shit, what the hell is wrong with me?" She bit out in frustration.

For the last few days, she'd come home from the charity's office, ready to go to bed and sleep the sleep of the dead. She had dreams she knew aroused her to a fever pitch, but when she awoke, she couldn't remember any details. No matter how she tried to remember the face of the man who drove her wild, it was always out of reach. Neither could she understand why her body ached as if she'd been fighting. She just couldn't remember a thing. It was like grasping at air made straws! She had no bruises to show for it and when she stared at her telescopic baton she'd have a memory flash which immediately disappeared. She didn't like this feeling. With a vicious twist of the tap, she got out of the shower and got dressed for work.

Volunteering, which she normally looked forward to and loved didn't give her a respite that day either. Her job was to keep the computer systems updated, yet for the life of her she couldn't understand why she couldn't remember the simple procedures. Panic gripped her. God, she was too young to have dementia! She made a beeline towards the Charity Officer's nook and told him she needed to take the next two weeks off. She had to find out what was wrong with her. It was just a good thing Kids Come Home was the charity she and Devon had formed. Devon was the public face of the charity. However, she didn't want anyone to know she was the silent partner.

Devon had been a down and out solicitor whom Eirene saved from a group of thugs. She had gotten him back on his feet after he'd been living in the rough for years. The whole time Devon was in hospital it was Eirene who visited him. They were two people who had no one else left in the world. Eirene's adoptive parents couldn't wait for her to turn eighteen before she was asked to leave. Devon's wife took their only daughter, Penny, away and disappeared, leaving him to pick up the pieces of his shattered life. Fate must have decided enough was enough and dealt them both a fair hand. Each other.

A woman wanting the love of a parent and a parent looking for a missing daughter.

Eirene made a deal with Devon. If he got off the streets and practiced law, she would be his first client. She would also help him find his daughter. Devon had agreed. He turned his life around, renewed his membership with the Law Society, and with Eirene's help, rebuilt his practice from the ground up. The newly recharged solicitor wasted no time hiring Henry Heaton, an expensive private investigator to look for his missing daughter. Finding Penny was what galvanized Eirene and Devon to establish the charity, Kids Come Home. They both decided they would try to help desperate and bereft parents look for their missing children. The funds they raised from Eirene's programming, as well as from several fundraisers, were used to hire several private detectives to track the whereabouts of abducted or runaway kids. Some of the reunions were happy.

Most were not.

As soon as Eirne entered her house she felt a wave of lethargy come over her. Straining against the odd desire to sleep, she entered her bedroom and walked straight to the bathroom to take a cold shower.

"Holy shiiit!" She squealed at the ice cold spray, staying underneath the arctic blast until she could no longer bear it, then adjusted the temperature as soon as the vestiges of drowsiness disappeared. Feeling more normal and ready to do an all-nighter, she climbed the stairs to her loft office to check on the programs she'd developed for existing clients.

This was her favorite place in her house. Eirene had the loft insulated from the heat and cold, which made it an ideal workplace. She walked towards the blinds and drew them to the sides of the dark tinted windows. She swung the windows open. Summer was giving way to autumn. The air was cooler. There was a nip in the air and the faint smell of drying leaves.

A low leather cream couch with an Aztec design throw over the back was pushed against the brick wall opposite the door. There was a low coffee table which was, at the moment, strewn with several computer magazines. A book on semiotics rested on top of the bookshelf, tucked into the far wall. The computer and CCTV table was made from one long plank of polished cherry wood which was affixed to the brick wall. Eirene flicked a switch beside it and seconds later, the deceptively soft whir of monitor fans filled the silence of the room. She typed in her password before walking to the opposite end of the room to brew some coffee.

Finally, sitting down with a mug of hot java, Eirene went through the footage of the night she couldn't remember. She sipped her beverage, patiently waiting for something to show up when her land line rang. She turned to the small credenza to her left and reached for the portable phone. She checked the number and saw it was Devon. She already knew why Devon was calling. They had a very persistent client who wanted to meet the person behind the repair programs. But this particular client was different. The code of their system was the one which had the unusual symbols of "S" and

"C" embedded in the script, and it was the reason why Eirene had been able to infiltrate their system.

"They want to meet you." Devon said without preamble. "Have you finished the program?"

"You know that's not gonna happen and I just need to put it a few more codes before it's done. I'm not quite sure it will work though. This has been the most difficult program I've made yet." Eirene said, giving a small chuckle at the phone as though Devon could see her. "That's why you're there for me. Remember, you're the public face of the company. I am the one in the shadows and I want to stay that way."

Devon's sigh sounded over the phone line, a sign that he was relenting. "Okay."

Eirene wanted to tell him about infiltrating this system and how promising it looked. She wanted to tell him about the possibility that this client might be hiding something and made sure that not even the authorities would be able to crack the system's code. But that would get Devon's hopes up of finding Penny, and if they found nothing, Eirene knew it would break Devon's heart.

"Devon, you know I can accomplish more when I remain anonymous," she said instead. "Have they paid the last tranche?"

"I have an appointment with them later today. They want to know how you were able to hack into their system."

"I'm not a hacker," she sniffed. "I infiltrate."

Devon chuckled. "They sound synonymous to me."

Eirene scowled at the phone but couldn't help the smile that teased her mouth.

"Oh, go on then."

The solicitor laughed. "They said their system was different from any other system. I think they were under the mistaken impression that it was impossible for anyone to infiltrate it."

"Yes, the code they used is nothing that I've seen before," she agreed, her mouth still twitching with amusement. "But I was able to get in."

"Are you willing to let them know how you were able to do so?"

Eirene tsked. "That would be divulging company secrets."

Devon chuckled. "Don't I know it. Be that as it may, could you still come over? Not that I would be introducing you to them," he added hastily before Eirene could say anything. "There's something about these people that I can't quite put my finger on."

"Like?"

"They give me the creeps, Eirene," he said, his voice a little troubled. "That's saying a lot coming from someone who has lived on the streets for almost five years."

"And how is my being there going to help?"

"I just don't want to be alone in the office. They have asked that the exchange be made at ten tonight."

Eirene's eyebrows rose. "At ten in the evening? That is unusual."

"Please be here, Eirene. You can always pretend to be the cleaning lady."

Eirene laughed. "You've thought of my disguise like you know I'll agree."

"Please?"

"Okay, okay! Stop being such a whiner. You're a middle aged solicitor for heaven's sake. Solicitors don't whine."

This time Devon laughed. "You don't know the half of it. Thanks, chuck."

"Where do I get my disguise?"

"I'll leave it in the cleaner's closet. That way no one will think we know each other."

After she ended the call, Eirene looked at the wall clock above her console desk. It was just six in the evening. Plenty of time to run through the CCTV and arrive at Devon's with time to spare. She went back to scrutinizing the CCTV footage. No one knew she had installed cameras around her house. The security devices were embedded in between the grooves of her house's siding. They were tiny cameras which looked like they were part of the plaster but had strong lenses which could focus sharply on their query.

There! She frowned in concentration as she saw herself enter the house. Several minutes later she saw two men stop in front of her door. Eirene's heart raced. She stared at one of the men. She knew him, but she didn't know how or why. She screamed in frustration, angry at herself for not being able to remember anything except the heat of a man's body by her side before he moved to face her. As though her body was separate from her mind, it remembered how having that male body next to hers made her feel. It brought warmth to her cheeks and delicious shivers down her spine and to her quim. She closed her eyes to remember his scent, but when she tried to grasp the memory it moved away from her like mist. She rubbed her forehead in irritation and stared again at the CCTV monitor. She couldn't understand why the camera could clearly display her face but couldn't focus on the faces of the men. It was odd, as if the camera wanted to hide their identities. Then the unthinkable happened.

They entered her house.

"Oh my God." Eirene uttered, as she stiffened before moving her chair forward. Her eyes widened in confusion and fear.

Mesmerized, Eirene watched and waited, her stomach tied into knots. Two men had entered her house and she had no idea who they were. Suddenly she started to shake. She gripped her hands together to try and stop the tremors of shock which wracked her body. Less than five minutes later both men left the house. Only the man she could vaguely remember stopped to turn and look at her door before he followed his companion.

Eirene slumped in her chair as her heart knocked about inside her chest. What the hell happened that night? Why couldn't she remember? Who were these men? How were they able to get through the alarm system without waking the neighbours or even triggering the panic button of her security system provider? Cold dread spread through her. Had they touched her? Did they drug her so she wouldn't remember the despicable things they did to her? Surely her body would have remembered any violation even if her mind could not. Her heart plummeted when she remembered how sore she felt. Was it because she was not in a fight but was really violated? Had she been raped?

As Eirene stood, her knees nearly buckled underneath her and a wave of nausea hit right in the pit of her stomach. Sucking in her breath she imposed an iron control on herself and she forced her legs to hold her steady. She exhaled slowly. She took tentative steps and in no time at all began to pace the length of the office. She clenched and unclenched her hands to release her tension. Devon might be able to help. She would show him the footage and they'd take it from there. In the meantime, her friend needed her. She grabbed her mobile phone, her telescopic baton and her keys before she walked out the door.

CHAPTER FOUR

Finn stayed in the shadows as he watched the rare Mercedes S65 stop in front of the St James' Building along Oxford Road. The art deco edifice gleamed dully like the colour of bone against the dull orange lamplight. He looked up at the building. Only the penthouse was flooded with lights this late at night. Oxford Road looked almost deserted of people walking on the pavement. The flower shop, New York Deli and cafes by the sides of the building's façade were closed with only a few fluorescent bulbs to ward off the dark.

The driver got out and circled to the other side to open the passenger door. Finn inhaled sharply, disbelief running through him. Finn knew the man who exited the car was Scatha Cruor. He had seen him before. What he didn't expect was the other man who joined him. The Scatha's companion was the one man the entire Cynn Cruor had been hunting for almost a thousand years.

Dac Valerian. When he was in Caesar's army he was known as General Gnaeus Valerius Dacronius.

Finn had no time to lose. He'd call Roarke while he followed his quarry. His mission was to find out where the rest of the Scatha Cruor were hiding, and Dac needed to remain alive for the Cynn Cruor to find out that information. Finn also needed to know where they were heading because he might never get another chance like this. If he caught them, it could mean the end of the thousand year old war between the Cynn Cruor and the Scatha Cruor, and it could happen tonight.

Finn crossed the street in a blur, just a few inches away from the oncoming Stagecoach bus. The driver did not see a thing. Finn would appear like a newspaper page being tossed by a sudden breeze onto the pavement. His all black outfit of leather jacket, shirt and jeans made him blend with the shadows. No one noticed him jump up to the top of the building. He zoomed to the fire exit and let himself in. The Scatha Cruor would take their time arriving at their destination. They needed to pretend to be like the rest of the populace. But unlike the Cynn Cruor, the evil which polluted their blood had addled their brains. They wouldn't realize a Cynn Cruor was nearby until it was too late.

Finn tracked them. They were on the second floor. He zinged towards the lit offices. The name *Devon and Spence Law Offices* was emblazoned in gold lettering on the glass doors. With all the offices in the building unlit, his gut instinct told him this was where Dac and his companion were heading.

He entered without making a sound. It did not matter that he was caught on CCTV. His image would be a blurry blob. His brow arched as he looked around. Either Devon and Spence did not care about the high cost of electricity or they had loads of money to burn. He heard the whirring sound of a vacuum cleaner as he rounded the reception area to enter the inner offices. The corridor was empty, save for a lone cleaning woman vacuuming the carpet, earphones stuck to her ears. Finn felt the Scatha Cruor's presence. They had arrived. He quickly entered one of the unlit offices when the buzzer in the reception area hummed.

From the far end of the hallway, a door swished open, revealing a middle aged man in an expensive shirt and trousers. The light overhead shone over his receding hairline. His face was tired, but apprehensive. He tapped the cleaning lady on the shoulder. She switched off the vacuum. Finn's sharp hearing allowed him to eavesdrop on their conversation.

"They're here," the man said as he fidgeted with his tie.

The woman nodded.

"I'll be close," she said. "It will be alright, Devon."

Finn harshly took a quick intake of breath. It couldn't be. But after three nights of not being able to stop thinking of her, he would recognize that voice anywhere. Warmth seeped through him like honey. Her voice was soft and sweet with a hint of steel. Just as he remembered it. It wasn't a voice he would have associated with a cleaning lady. Seeing her now in the bright lights of the office, he wondered what she was doing here. Perhaps she was working for extra money? Or maybe she was a friend of the solicitor? What kind of solicitor would speak to a cleaning lady to tell her that his clients had arrived even before meeting them? And what kind of cleaning lady would assure her employer things would be alright? Did they know the true identities of their visitors?

Something wasn't right about the whole setup. He cussed under his breath. Anytime the Scatha Cruor were involved, danger was as evident and unmistakable as a neon sign. He just never expected the female in the park to be in the office dressed as the cleaning woman.

Finn deftly removed his mobile phone from his jacket pocket. He was too far from the Faesten to telepathically send a message to his fellow warriors. For once he wished he was a full blooded vampire, so he could communicate with his brethren regardless of the distance.

"St James' Place. Top floor. Bring the team," he said before he ended the call.

The man called Devon approached the entrance. Finn heard the exchange of pleasantries before Devon returned with Dac and his companion walking behind him. Finn felt the familiar anger that seethed through his veins at the sight of the Cynn Cruor's nemesis. His whole body screamed for revenge and it took all of his willpower to stamp it down. His eyes honed on the strongest Scatha Cruor alive. Finn knew he had the advantage of surprise. If he didn't kill the Scatha, the Scatha would kill him. The problem was he also needed to know where the rest were hiding. If the Cynn Cruor killed the Scatha Cruor leader without knowing where the rest of his followers were, the war still wouldn't end.

Finn almost choked at the stench of evil which surrounded the two men like stagnant air over a garbage dump. It was the one thing he hated about fighting the Scatha. Their smell of sewage and detritus was so rancid that not even their expensive colognes could mask the scent. After hundreds of years, he still wasn't used to it.

Devon entered one of the bigger meeting rooms, switched on the lights and held the door as the men walked in. He told them to make themselves comfortable while he got what they came for. Finn's sharp eyes surveyed the area. The cleaning lady was nowhere to be seen. So much for being close by. He would find her.

Later.

Devon returned with a small flat container the size of a cigarette case. He handed this to the Scatha leader.

"I believe you have something for me as well," Devon stated.

"We need to check if the program works first," Dac replied.

"Of course," the solicitor said nodding.

The Scatha's companion produced a laptop which he switched on. He took out the USB from the case and slotted it in, waiting for the program to run.

"I was hoping to meet the genius who made this. It's very interesting how our firewall was hacked," Dac commented.

Devon arched a brow. "Kids nowadays have a capacity to learn computer languages beyond anything we older ones could imagine. Firewalls mean very little to them. I guess it's the fast pace of technology which makes today's newest gadget almost obsolete even before it hits a store's shelves."

"Ahh, but our firewall and system are very unique." Dac's eyes narrowed. "It's fool proof. Until the brains behind this program came along."

"Then it's probably not as fool proof as you think."

From Finn's vantage point, he saw Dac's jaw tighten in anger, but the solicitor was oblivious to it. Or trying to be. Finn's vampire blood sensed the rush of fear in the pulse that ticked sporadically against Devon's temple even though the middle aged solicitor appeared unruffled.

Dac gave Devon a humourless smile.

"Is there anything I can do to meet this genius?"

Devon shook his head with regret.

"You are very persistent, Mr. Valerian, but it really isn't possible. Not one of my clients has seen this person. And as this genius is also one of my clients, I am duty bound not to divulge anything. Solicitor-client confidentiality and all that, you understand."

"You are quite a clever man, Mr. Devon. Not even revealing whether this genius is male or female. And please, call me Dac."

"Client confidentiality extends to that courtesy, Mr. Dac."

Dac remained unperturbed, but his eyes narrowed.

"I could use someone with this kind of talent in my organization. The perks of the job are second to none. The latest and most expensive car as a gift even before work begins, then a house or a flat of the person's choice and a fat bank account. More than what your client probably makes in a year."

"I will let my client know of your offer," Devon said. "Although, I can say right now they won't be interested."

Dac stood up and took a step towards Devon. His companion glanced at them with a smirk. Finn felt the waves of trepidation roll off the solicitor.

"I can be very persuasive," Dac spoke, his voice soft and dangerous.

"It's working," his companion spoke.

Dac pivoted and moved to look at the laptop's monitor with excitement.

"Excellent!"

The cloud of danger and evil which seemed to swirl like a black mist around them immediately disappeared. Dac looked at Devon.

"The last payment will be sent via bank transfer when I get to meet the genius behind the program."

Devon's eyes widened before he frowned his displeasure.

"That wasn't our agreement."

Dac laughed. "I've just changed our agreement."

"You're breaking the contract just to meet my other client?" Devon asked in consternation. "I told you that wasn't possible."

Dac sighed and tutted.

He shrugged. "Then you don't get paid."

Devon didn't hide his annoyance.

"Perhaps you don't understand the laws here. You're in breach of our contract. I have no compunction about hauling you to court," Devon warned. His face was red and a thick vein on his neck was close to turning purple.

Finn saw that Dac's companion had noticed the vein and saw the hunger in his eyes. Finn hissed. He couldn't let the Scatha give in to their desire for human blood. Neither could he blow his cover. With Dac around, he would need his brethren. Dammit! He wanted to kill Dac so badly, he could taste it as bitter bile in his mouth. He had to diffuse the danger to the solicitor's life quickly, because Dac was using his skill to bend Devon's mind to his will.

"That's it, Mr. Devon." Dac soothed the agitated man, while his companion slowly moved towards the solicitor rooted to the spot.

"To hell with this," Finn muttered but even before he could move, the entire floor was plunged into darkness. Finn's sensitive hearing heard a sucking sound before a shrill sound pierced his ears. Even Dac and his companion yowled in pain. Then the glass walls and doors of the meeting room imploded. Shrieks of pain and anger reverberated around the room as glass shattered. Several shards embedded themselves on the Scatha Cruor's exposed skin.

"Run Devon!"

Finn heard the female voice and was momentarily immobilized.

Finn eyes adjusted to the dark. He saw her swing her baton at Dac's companion, who was carrying the box with the USB. The stick bore down hard on his hand and he screamed in fury. She grabbed the box and was about to flee when Dac's hand snaked out and caught her.

* * * *

Eirene screamed when she felt a hand—no, a claw—grab her hair. She thought her hair would be pulled right out of her scalp. Her stomach heaved at the stench she smelled underneath the expensive cologne. It smelled of sewage and stale sweat and it was coming from the man's skin. She shuddered in disgust, her heart fluttering in fear when she felt him sniff her, then lick her nape. His smell was familiar, but she couldn't quite remember where she'd smelled it before. She struggled, trying to twist around to whack him on the head with her baton, but the hold on her hair was excruciating and she dared not risk moving for fear of literally having her hair torn out by the roots.

"I like the smell and taste of your fear," the man said, his voice guttural. But before he could do anything more, Eirene heard a feral growl before it launched itself at her attacker, pushing her away.

Eirene didn't wait to see who or what it was that came to her aid. Instead, she sprinted to where Devon lay. He moaned, moving his head from side to side, but remained unconscious. Eirene looked back at the fray. A man's figure stood out of the shadows, fighting the men Devon had spoken to earlier, but he looked outgunned. Both men were attacking him simultaneously. She had to do something. Then she remembered the piercing whistle she used to break the glass. She fumbled in her pockets and grabbed it. She pressed down hard on the button. The men snarled, momentarily stopping the brawl.

"Let's go," her attacker spoke harshly to his companion, covering their ears as they whizzed out of the office at an unbelievable speed. She turned to look at the man left behind. She released the button and the man fell on all fours.

"Did you have to keep your finger on the button? My ears are killing me," he growled.

Eirene's eyes widened, then she frowned in irritation.

"You're welcome, you ungrateful asshole," she muttered. Standing up, she left the room to switch on the lights from the fuse box inside the janitorial room. The first thing she saw when she returned was the man's back as he easily carried Devon to his office and lay him gently on the leather sofa, flushed against the left wall of the office. He straightened up and turned to face her. Her eyes widened.

"You!"

This man was Finn Qualtrough.

Suddenly, everything she hadn't been able to remember in almost seventy-two hours came back to her in a rush. Air whooshed out of her as though she took a kick in the gut. She walked backwards until she felt the bookshelf behind her. She gripped the lip of a low shelf to keep herself upright. Panic seared through her while she felt something else, something more.

Betrayal.

His midnight blue eyes bored into hers. Even with her body suffused with anger and humiliation, his eyes still sent a message that seared her insides with an aching need. She sucked in her breath at the intense arousal she felt. It made her stomach quiver, her knees weak, and her womanhood throb. His pupils dilated like he knew the effect he had on her. Eirene saw tiny gold flecks appear in his eyes. They sent shafts of desire through her entire being. Even with his body several feet away from hers, she could feel his heat as if he was just a few inches away. She had never met a man who would ignite her body the way he did. Just being near him sent her imagination into overdrive. In her mind's eye she felt his hands caress her again, shape and cup her breasts before his mouth sucked and worshiped her nipples. That was what had happened in the park. Her mind stung with the memory of her shame. He had rejected her.

Finn took a step toward her.

"Don't," she choked. Her throat was so dry, she thought she wouldn't be able to swallow.

She finally remembered.

Everything.

CHAPTER FIVE

The swish of the front glass door broke their connection. Eirene exhaled slowly, belatedly realizing that she'd been holding her breath the whole time. She turned to see who had arrived, her stance defensive as she backed away from Devon's office door. Four hunks appeared and entered the office one at a time. All of them were as tall as Finn, their jeans riding low on their hips. Their black shirts skimmed and hugged their muscled chests and washboard abs. They were also wearing leather jackets in different styles. The third man to come in had a satchel slung over his shoulder. He strode immediately towards Devon.

"Stop! You're not going anywhere near him." Eirene placed herself between Devon, Finn and the man with a satchel.

"Zac is a doctor," the man who appeared to be their leader said. "If you don't allow him near your friend, his injuries will only get worse."

Eirene briefly hesitated, looking at all of them warily. Finally, she conceded moving to one side to allow the man called Zac to kneel before Devon and start cleaning his wounds.

"We have not been properly introduced," the man said, his silver blue eyes crinkling int friendliness, the corners of his mouth lifting to a smile. "Roarke Hamilton."

"I very much doubt you were really planning on introducing yourself to me before." Eirene gave an unladylike snort.

There was a sudden fit of chuckled coughing from Roarke's two other companions.

"Graeme Temple." A man with wavy dark brown hair and gray green eyes extended his hand. Eirene hesitated before she gave his hand a quick shake.

"And this joker here is Blake Strachan." Roarke's mouth lifted to give her a lopsided grin. "Zac McBain is our resident medic. And the man whose life you saved three nights ago is Finn Qualtrough."

At the mention of her saving Finn's life, dusky rose heat crested her cheeks at the remembrance of what happened between them. She could feel Finn's eyes on her, but she refused to look at him. Didn't he know it was rude to give her that sexy look in front of his friends?

Finn moved closer to her and Eirene snapped her head around to look at him.

"And she saved me again tonight, though my ears took a bashing."

"So you're the female who helped kill the Scatha," Blake said, slightly awed.

Eirene's gaze swung to him. "Better them than me."

Blake chuckled before looking at Finn.

Finn's left-sided grin was the most devastating smile Eirene had ever seen on a man. His perfectly formed and sensuous mouth was made for kissing. Eirene's own mouth tingled at the memory of his lips on hers.

"I never got to thank you."

"No need," she said, her body heating under his gaze.

"Finn, we need to know what happened here." Roarke spoke, breaking the sexual tension between them. "We couldn't get up here as fast as we could with that shrill bell."

Finn appeared to reluctantly shift his gaze to Roarke.

"Dac was here."

Eirene was startled by the numerous swear words

that fell like rain over her head.

"Hold it! My ears are ringing with all of you cussing." She made the "T" sign with her hands as she scowled. She still clutched the baton in her right fist. A trickle of trepidation skittered all over her body when she saw their eyes turn to red orange, like the dying rays of the sun. Except for Finn, whose eyes remained a sexy midnight blue.

Roarke looked at her. Soon, the fury in his eyes began to ebb, returning to its silver blue color. He raked his hand through his hair as he gave her a brief smile.

"Sorry," he said. "We've been searching for Dac for a very long time and this has been the closest we have ever gotten to him."

"And how long is a long time?" she asked. Her pulse began to race again because she knew she was treading on deadly ground. She had a strong suspicion that they weren't exactly human and again she couldn't understand why she could accept them for who they were and not scream bloody murder. She swallowed hard remembering the way their eyes changed but their faces didn't. At least they smelled really good, especially Finn. It was as though her nasal passages wanted to make a beeline and take all of his smell into her body. Eirene wanted to sigh, the longing so strong inside her that she wished all except Finn remained in the room. They exuded danger and yet she felt safe.

"Please, tell me," she spoke again. "How long is a long time?"

Everyone was quiet. Roarke's face was devoid of emotion as he continued to stare at her.

Eirene bit her lip before speaking. "Maybe way before I was born?"

Eirene heard Finn's sharp intake of breath and she became the cynosure of five pairs of eyes. Her heart seemed to thunder towards the center of her chest. She looked at Finn, then Roarke, then at everyone else. She inhaled deeply before expending her breath. She looked at both Finn and Roarke.

"You, Finn fought those monsters with me. And you, Roarke, you were the man I spoke with on the phone. You both came into my home." She paused. "I remember everything."

* * * *

"No way!"

"That's not possible!"

Graeme and Blake exclaimed at the same time. Zac quirked his mouth in a smile even as he continued to tend to Devon.

Finn's heart thudded. Hard. Roarke looked at him barely containing his own disbelief.

How could this slip of a girl, no, woman break the thrall? And Finn knew she was one hell of a woman. He could still remember the night he had to keep her quiet and cover their scent so that the Scatha chasing her would not find her. The moment when he had pulled her close to his chest, had given him the time to experience her womanly curves, and his hardening arousal had nestled in between the cheeks of her pert ass. He remembered the feel of her ribcage and the underside of her breasts when he had held his arm around her and the taste of her nipple when he'd suckled her.

Her clothes moulded her form like second skin, and Finn wanted to lift her top to skim his palm over her silken flesh, to feel it heat under his touch, for it to quiver and crave his hand again and again. His own lips wanted to savor her lips again. His tongue wanted to delve into the sweet recesses of her mouth to entice her tongue to come out and play. And her breasts. Ancients!

They filled his palm, her nipples jutting out like pouts, wanting to be spoiled by his mouth.

After he and Roarke had left her house to wipe her memory that night, they returned to the Faesten. The short kiss Finn shared with Eirene hadn't been adequate to heal him after the Scatha's swipe of his chest and his use of the gift of cloaking. So he had slept. The first time in his entire immortal life, he had slept at night. When he'd awoken several hours later, he had been disoriented until he remembered her. It was her body and her scent he had remembered the most. The scent of honey mixed with the scent of her growing arousal when he'd kissed her. In the park, he'd had to fight the impulse to take a nip of her, to taste her blood or take her right then and there. When he'd held her body close to his it had just felt so right, as though she was made for him. Even now, he regretted the night had ended badly.

Because he wanted her.

He wanted to get to know her body, to see what it felt like to be inside of her. He had never sought a woman or even regretted losing one as much as when she had walked away from him in the park that night. He'd been on the hunt to kill evil. Instead, he had found something perplexing, but beautiful. Sensual.

Now she was here. In close proximity to him.

And his cock jerked in greeting.

"What's not possible?" she asked.

"You...remembering," Blake blurted, sweeping both his hands over his cropped hair, disturbing the soft spiky edges at the top of his head. He looked at her bemusedly. "What did you do?"

"I went through CCTV footage..."

"Not even looking through CCTV could trigger your memory," Graeme scoffed. He paused. "You have

CCTV?"

Roarke expelled his breath, his impatience showing on his face. "The more we delay, the farther Dac will be."

"Who's Dac? And you haven't answered my question," she scowled.

After a moment's hesitation, Roarke approached her. Finn made a move to go to her when she flicked her telescopic baton.

"Stay right where you are," she warned, her eyes narrowed at all of them, her stance defensive. This woman was willing to take on all of them, even if she knew the odds were against her. Damn, that was sexy. Incredible.

And beautiful.

"There are shards of glass in your hair," Roarke said quietly.

"I'll do it," Finn said, moving in a blur. He completely forgot she had intended to fight them, yet she didn't move away when he drew near. Did she just almost lean towards him?

Just like on the night he had first met her, Finn noticed she was all in black.

Her shoulder length hair shone blue black underneath the soft glow of the office lights. Black hipster jeans skimmed and hugged her slim runner's legs and gave more definition to her sexy ass. Her tank top fit her flat stomach, shaping her narrow waist, and covered round firm breasts like a glove. Her toned arms were tense as one hand held the baton and the other clenched into a fist. Finn raked his gaze over her graceful neck, her oval face filled with trepidation, and yet there was a strong determination in her sable coloured baby doll eyes. They were fringed with sooty lashes which did not need the help of any mascara. Finn saw her pert nose slightly flare as she inhaled and exhaled. And those lips, softly parted now, were rosy and delectable. Finn coughed as he held back the groan that wound its way up his throat. How he wanted to taste her again. To feel her. To explore her languidly until she peaked in his arms. He always found pleasure in making women climax, but watching this woman shatter in orgasm would be indescribable. If she gave him a chance, he wanted to make it up to her. Finn wanted a second chance.

Why did it matter to him what this female thought of him? Why did a part of him want to linger around her longer than was necessary? Why did he want her to accept him even if he wasn't entirely human?

"Why don't you sit down," he said after brushing away the tiny slivers of glass from her hair. "We're not here to hurt you."

Finn noticed her flinch slightly when he touched her elbow and wondered why that movement hit him like a blow.

Eventually, her grip on the baton relaxed. She brought her weapon to her side and sat down. Without a moment's hesitation, Finn sat beside her on the sofa. He gave her a brief smile before looking at the rest of the Cynn Cruor, his eyes challenging them. Graeme and Blake looked at each other and shrugged. Roarke's mouth quirked in amusement.

"Seeing that wiping your memory didn't work, I have no intention of doing so again," Roarke said with mock brevity as he arched a brow. He turned towards Devon's desk to lean on it with his arms crossed over his chest. "But before we answer your questions, we need to know your name. You do have one, don't you?"

"Why?" She didn't answer Roarke.

Blake chuckled. "Well, do you want to be called

'hey you'?"

Her scowl slowly disappeared and her lips pressed into a thin line before they lifted.

"Point taken," she said. She hesitated before she spoke, "Eirene. Spence."

"As in the Spence on the glass door outside?" Graeme inclined his head towards the entrance.

"Yes. That Spence." Her voice was so soft that if it hadn't been for his superior hearing, Finn would not have heard her. The name Eirene suited her. It meant peace. Something inside him stirred. Was Eirene the person to give him the peace he'd been seeking for his entire immortal life? He wondered if she was capable of driving his demons away.

"So, how long have you been looking for this Dac guy?" Eirene queried. "And please don't give me any bullshit, because I have a pretty good idea of what you all are."

After a moment's hesitation, Roarke nodded. "Fair enough. We have been looking for him for almost a thousand years."

Eirene's eyes rounded, her mouth agape.

"So...that makes all of you..." Eirene cleared her throat. "Uh....uhhmm."

"We're not that old," Blake muttered with a scowl. "At least, I'm not."

"We were born in different centuries, but we don't age," Finn explained. "We have been looking for Dac so we can end the war between our kinds. The Cynn Cruors and the Scatha Cruors."

When Eirene turned to look at him, Finn wanted to cup her face and trace her lips with his thumb, and then with his mouth. Her eyes bored into his as though she was looking straight into his soul to see if they were all speaking the truth. If she saw all the things he'd had to do to protect his kin, he wondered what she would think. In the end, he broke the intense contact with her and looked down at his hands clasped between his knees.

That's a first. Finn heard Zac telepathically tell him.

Shut up, Finn retorted.

Graeme and Blake looked down to hide their grins. Roarke eyed him steadily.

"The Cynn Cruors?" Eirene searched their faces, her eyes mirroring her confusion. "Aren't you all vampires?"

"And you're not afraid of us?" Zac inquired with slight surprise from where he knelt in front of Devon.

"Funnily enough, no. Don't' ask me to explain," she raised her hand to stop him. "Because I don't have any answer either. I just know that you are… that you exist. Hell, I might just be dreaming everything up." The moment those words left her lips she knew that all this couldn't possibly be a dream. Finn's kiss was a testament to that. The thought brought warmth glowing in her belly and heating her face.

Blake snickered and yelped when Graeme brought his elbow against his rib.

"We do have vampire blood in our veins, but we aren't vampires," Roarke answered. "We have both vampire and werewolf blood in our DNA. But we are also partly human."

"You can have both?" Eirene asked in surprise.

"Yes," Zac murmured from where he was treating Devon's wounds. "The DNA we have is collectively called the Kinaré gene."

"Our progenitor, the Ancient Eald also known as the Ancient Cynn was an alchemist. His knowledge of different magickal traditions was and still is unsurpassed," Finn answered. "He knew how to extract vampire and werewolf blood without being bitten or attacked. He took the better qualities of each blood and blended it with human blood, creating the Kinaré gene, thus creating the Cynn Cruors."

"I didn't think vampire or werewolf blood had any redeeming qualities," Eirene mused, almost to herself. "Why would he do that?"

"We don't know his reasons for doing so." Roarke said as he shifted his weight against the desk. "He chose several families to become Cynn Cruors. They have remained immortal. Obviously we need to be careful so that humans don't know who we are. We have lived peacefully among mortals, and have even helped spur new technologies in every civilization and time in history."

"The Cynn Eald used to get into debates with Plato and Sophocles. Other Cynn Cruor warriors disappeared from the scene after helping mortals with their discoveries, letting them take the credit." Finn added.

"Why?" Eirene asked.

"What do you think the world would do if they knew who we were? Our mortal colleagues would age, while we remained the same." Roarke countered. "Ponce de Leon never found the Fountain of Youth. What do you think they would do to us if they got hold of our blood?"

"We're not blood sucking fiends, or snarling, biting hairy curs." All eyes turned to Zac when he spoke. "The vampire part of the Kinaré gene makes us stronger than mortals and allows us mobility and agility close to the speed of light. We can communicate telepathically, but only when we are at close proximity with one another. We also see clearly in the dark as if it was daylight."

"And the werewolf blood?" She asked, her head inclined to one side.

"It adds to the strength we already have. It also makes us warm so that when you touch us, you won't realize we're different. It balances out the coldness of our vampire DNA." Zac replied. "Among other things…"

"What other things?" She prodded.

Graeme and Blake straightened.

"Blake and I will check the perimeter." Graeme said suddenly after clearing his throat. Eirene noticed Blake trying to stop a grin from lighting up his face.

Roarke nodded to them before they left.

"We can't stay here any longer." Roarke pushed himself from the desk. "Dac knows we're here. We need to get back to the Faesten."

"We have to take Devon to the hospital first." Eirene said as she stood up. She looked down at the unconscious solicitor. Most of Devon's wounds had been cleaned, but blood still continued to trickle from the deeper cuts.

"We will have to bring your friend with us." Zac said as he took one last look at Devon.

"Why not the hospital?"

"Like the Cynn, the Scatha are everywhere." Finn replied. "Dac also knows what you look like. He will be able to find you."

"The lights were off."

Finn arched his brow.

"Oh right. Your vampire blood," she grumbled. She knelt, facing Devon. Zac stood and stepped back. Eirene held Devon's limp hand in hers and squeezed. She remained pensive for several moments. Her hair fell down her shoulders and partly rested on her breast. Finn's hands itched to cup those perfect globes again. That brief taste of her body had sent lust spiralling down his spine and into his member. Just thinking of the moments he had spent nursing at her breast sent new signals to his surprisingly wayward appendage. Clenching his jaw, he steeled himself to stop thinking of

Eirene naked. He didn't want to walk with a tent between his thighs.

"I can't just disappear." Eirene said in an almost helpless whisper. She straightened and turned to look at Roarke, Zac and Finn.

"We're not asking you to." Roarke replied before his face hardened. "Please, we have to go. We will answer all your questions once we are safely inside the Faesten."

Finn turned her to face him.

"I will protect you," he said. "I give you my word."

"Can someone else take me instead?"

Finn felt like he'd been slapped. He felt the heat rise up his face, remorse filling him.

"There is no one else, Eirene." Roarke said. "Zac has to take care of Devon and I have to report to the Council of Ieldran. Everything is time sensitive. You have my word that Finn will take care of you. He is my second."

Finn exhaled slowly. The dull ache in his chest which he'd felt that night in the park returned. He had to consciously stop himself from rubbing the spot over his heart.

Eirene looked at him. His stomach clenched, not wanting to accept the emotion he saw flit through her eyes.

Distrust.

Then, she reluctantly nodded.

"Alright," she said while exhaling. "But you owe me big time. All of you."

Roarke nodded. "We'll take the solicitor back to the Faesten. Finn, take a different route and keep Eirene safe. Zac take the SUV. I will meet you in the Faesten." He took out his mobile phone and spoke to Graeme to get the SUV ready.

Zac slung his satchel across his shoulder and

positioned it against his back. Gently he carried the unconscious man in his arms before he and Roarke left.

"Let's go." Finn said, his voice brusque. If Eirene didn't want to have anything to do with him, he would respect her wishes. If only her rejection didn't smart. Why did Eirene have such an effect on him?

Eirene's cheeks turned a deeper shade of rose. She began moving about, tucking the baton in her back pocket. She left the room for a moment, then returned, shrugging into her black leather biker jacket, and strode towards Devon's desk.

"Eirene, what are you doing?"

"Give me a minute," she said as she typed on the keyboard.

Finn swore inwardly. This woman had a stubborn streak. Problem was, he liked it. A lot. He followed her and looked at the monitor. Eirene was transferring files to a cloud drive.

"This is taking too much time," she muttered, her brown eyes intent on what was happening in front of her.

Finn closed his eyes. He could sense the Scatha near. With reluctance, he harnessed his gift of cloaking, a gift any Cynn Cruor had. This was the second time he had ever used it during his entire existence, and both times involved Eirene. He knew that using the gift would take a lot of his strength from him, especially since this was a bigger place, comprising almost the entire floor. Compared to this, the area of Shakespearean Gardens where he had protected Eirene was a little over a quarter of the office.

He felt heat emanate from the centre of his chest. Like a tentacle of white smoke, the gift created a web of clear air which surrounded him and Eirene. It shimmered for a moment before it settled to nothingness. The Scatha would not be able to smell them, nor could they be seen inside the room.

Dimly, Finn heard a soft ping. He opened his eyes and saw that the last files on Devon's computer had been deleted. Eirene took out a USB and inserted it into the USB slot. She executed the command to run, and in less than a minute she removed the USB.

"Let's go." Eirene said, but stopped. She gripped his hand in hers. Finn felt her fear like tar in a bog.

There was a commotion coming from the reception area of the office. Eirene turned fearful eyes to him. Finn sighed.

"Now you know why we had to hurry," he whispered into her ear. He felt her shudder. "Put your arms around me and unless you want to die, you will do as I say."

Finn saw a wave of irritation flit through her eyes before it disappeared.

"Please, I need to go home before you take me to wherever you're supposed to take me," she whispered. "It's very important. And it might help you find Dac."

Finn stifled a groan. He wasn't quite sure anymore whether it was because of his exasperation or because Eirene's body was moulded against his. There was no way she would miss his growing arousal. He heard her suck in her breath, but she didn't utter a word.

The Scatha entered Devon's office. Finn heard Eirene's gasp but before Dac's followers could do anything, he swirled them both out of the window, speeding through Oxford Road in a blur.

CHAPTER SIX

Eirene didn't know whether the leap from Devon's office window or the fact that her body had been encased in Finn's arms was what made her pulse race and her body ignite. She closed her eyes, taking in the scent of a man and soap after a hot shower. A clean, sharp, and sexy smell. When he whispered in her ear, her body had quivered and trembled with a longing that had fuelled the ache in her core. She liked the sensations brought about by his muscled stomach and thighs pressed to hers. Her breasts felt heavy and needy against his ripped torso as his arm encircled her waist like a vice. She had felt his shaft growing hard against the crook of her hip even before they had jumped, and when he'd pressed his leg between her thighs to steady their landing, she had almost moaned. Eirene felt liquid arousal peek through her folds as her clitoris rubbed against his upper thigh.

So wrong, but so right, Eirene mused. It was always the case with her. She knew that when she had asked Roarke for someone else to keep her safe, she had humiliated Finn. A pang of guilt broke over her. Even after the fact, it seemed that the events in the park were making her do things she would never do otherwise. She knew what humiliation felt like and she had vowed to never make another person suffer the same crippling emotion.

Finn isn't human.

She looked up at him. Her cheeks warmed. Eirene wondered if he could tell how he affected her by just looking at her face. She tried to control her body's response to him. Impossible.

Now that she could see him clearly, Finn was ruggedly handsome. The soft breeze ruffled the short spikes of his haircut. He was nearly as muscled as Roarke. His black shirt moulded his body to perfection as his broad shoulders filled the jacket he wore. His stance underscored the strength of his thighs and his narrow hips that were hard against her body. Dark eyebrows slashed over midnight blue eyes that at the moment seemed to hold a hint of unforgotten pain. A generous, if not, sensual mouth, an aquiline nose, a straight forehead and perfectly chiselled high cheekbones completed a face so handsome, it could easily bring her to her knees.

"Are you alright?" Finn's deep timbre caressed her. Her heightened awareness of him seemed to attune her senses to his every move, his every expression. It made her want to hold him again and kiss him despite the fact she had vowed to never give in to that temptation again.

She heard him inhale sharply and when she looked into his face, Eirene almost melted at the hunger and desire she saw reflected in his eyes. Maybe if they shared one more kiss?

"We will. Later," Finn said. "I promise."

"God! You..." He had read her mind! Damn! She would have to monitor her every thought. Before she could say anything more, he scooped her in his arms. She held on tight with her cheek buried into the side of his neck. Oxford and Wilmslow Roads passed in a blur. In no time at all they were in Fallowfield, a residential area not far from the city's centre. Finn put her down slowly. Then he waited, his eyes holding a trace of amusement. Belatedly, Eirene realized that her arms were still around him. Reluctantly, she let him go, but his hands settled firmly on her waist.

"We're here, Eirene," Finn said softly. "Lead the way."

Eirene looked around to see they were by the

Shakespearean Gardens.

"Why are we here?" She asked in confusion. "You know where I live. Besides, you said we needed to leave quickly."

"I wanted to come back here to apologise for what happened," he said. "It wasn't supposed to end that way."

"That was almost three nights ago and you still think about it?" she asked softly as her gaze swept over his face.

Again in the dark, Eirene looked at his face, trying to see if there was any guile. There was none.

"Yes."

That one word sent a thrill that warmed her whole body. Excitement drummed through her at the knowledge that she wasn't the only one who had been affected by their encounter. Finn had not forgotten what it was like to kiss her. He had not forgotten what it was like to hold her. She saw his eyes look at the pulse at the base of her throat. God, how Eirene wanted him to lick her throat one more time. She wanted to bare it to his lips. More than anything, she wanted to return to that night and alter the ending.

"I see." She nodded and Finn stepped away from her, the heated imprint of his hands cooling on her waist. She looked at the direction from where they had come and wondered how much time they had.

"Don't worry. They won't know where we are because we're too far away now. Any Cynn Cruor who becomes a transfuge or traitor loses his tracking sense. Except for Dac. He used to be a Cynn Cruor before he became the leader of the Scatha Cruors. His Cynn Cruor faculties haven't deserted him, but he will be too busy trying to plot against us," Finn answered her unspoken question.

"Stop reading my mind." Eirene's brows knitted in a frown. She started walking, leaving him to follow. God, Finn must have read what she wanted to do to him. She cringed in embarrassment.

"I wasn't reading your mind, Eirene. It was obvious from your body language what you wanted to know." Finn fell into step beside her.

Eirene closed her eyes. What was happening to her? Every time he came near her she couldn't think straight. The sensual heat which rolled off his body teased her and she wanted to respond in the most erotic of ways. *Stop!* She scolded herself. *He can read minds remember?* She reddened when she heard him chuckle.

He leaned towards her and whispered in her ear.

"I made a promise earlier, Eirene Spence," he said, his voice deep and husky. "A Cynn Cruor never breaks his word."

"Yes, you did. You promised to keep me safe."

"And I promised to kiss you. Again."

She turned to him as she broke stride. "I didn't say anything!"

The lamplight along the deserted street caught Finn's eyes twinkling.

"True, but your mind did. Tell me I'm wrong," he added when she was about to deny it.

"I thought I told you to stop reading my mind."

"That was after you thought of me kissing you like I did when we first met."

Eirene's breath hitched. There was no point in denying it. From the moment he had rescued her she had wanted him. Wanted him with such an intensity it scared her, because she didn't know where this need came from. The last man she'd had a relationship with over a year ago had not made her feel this way. He hadn't made her yearn for him with every breath in her body.

Unlike Finn.

They continued to walk in silence until they turned onto Eirene's street. She fished out both her house and car keys from her jeans pocket, making a mental note to retrieve her car from the car park at Devon's office. She inserted the key into the lock, when she heard Finn emit a low growl. His chiselled features were partially hidden in the shadows and partly in sharp relief against the moonlit sky as he looked up. Then he looked back down at her. She gasped. His midnight blue eyes glowed with flecks of gold. It was something she had never seen before. Heart in her throat, Eirene tried to swallow, but she couldn't. Her mouth was suddenly dry. Heat burned her cheeks. She was breathless. Her body thrummed and trembled for the immortal beside her. His gaze skimmed over her and everywhere he looked, goose bumps trailed along her skin. When his gaze reached her breasts, her body arched involuntarily and she thrust her breasts towards him. She could feel her nipples harden. Just the thought of his mouth sucking on her, had her sex pulsing with need.

Finn closed the distance between them. He held her gaze, enthralling her. She placed her palm over his heart and a jolt of electricity zinged up her arm.

"Finn." her voice came out in a whisper. "I don't think…"

"You think this is wrong, Eirene?" He asked softly. Eirene closed her eyes and sighed while he tucked a strand of her hair behind her ear, then caressed her nape. She leaned into his palm as Finn's thumb caressed her lower lip. "Then why does it feel so right? Why do I long to kiss you? Why do I long to taste you, arouse your clit with my tongue and cover my mouth with your cream? Why do I want to lick you until you come again and again?"

"Oh God." Eirene breathed. Her heart was beating hard and fast. She bent her head to try to get her breathing under control. She moaned softly when Finn cupped her head under her hair and his thumb caressed the sensitive skin behind her ear.

"Let me make it up to you, Eirene. I want to apologize in the most decadent of ways."

Eirene's blood rejoiced and roared through her as her breath came in shorter pants. Her need overrode all coherent and rational thought. It didn't make sense for her to jump into bed with Finn, but her body begged, screamed even, to give in and let him ease the relentless hunger throbbing within her. It didn't matter that she hardly knew him or that he wasn't completely human. She wanted him. She wanted to lie underneath him, to straddle and ride him to oblivion until the world shattered around her and they were the only beings left on the planet. She did not have any illusions of this being permanent. She was getting out of her comfort zone. She never went for one-night stands, but this sensual being whose gaze singed her changed all of that. If this was only going to be a moment, one glorious moment that would keep her until the end of her days, she'd take it.

Eirene licked Finn's thumb as it brushed her lower lip and sucked it, her gaze riveted on him. The heady and slightly salty taste of his flesh brought a charge of desire down to her mound. Her mouth curved into a faint smile when he inhaled sharply.

"Tell me about the part of you that is werewolf," she spoke tentatively even as she continued to lick his digit. "Do you change form?"

Finn was breathing hard. Eirene turned her face into his palm and licked it. Finn gave a low growl.

"I will show you once we're inside."

Eirene looked at Finn and saw the desire in his eyes, fuelling her own. More liquid heat rushed to the apex between her thighs. She dragged her gaze away as Finn's hand let go of her face.

"Come in."

She welcomed him, entering the house with Finn close behind. Fumbling for the light switch, she heard the door click, but was startled when a warm hand covered hers.

"No, Eirene." Finn's mouth whispered into her ear. "I want you to feel what the moon does to us. To me."

Eirene stayed where she was. Finn made her face the wall. He took both her hands in one of his and brought them up above her head. He brought his body flushed against her back, his chest to her back, and his hip to her lower back. She gave a moaning sigh.

Her derriere was against a raging hard-on.

Her sex was wet with desire. She leaned back against his shoulder, moaning when he pushed his straining erection against her bottom. Finn bent down and licked the shell of her left ear, then gently nipped on the earlobe.

"Take your jacket off." Finn rasped. Eirene did as she was told, shrugging it from her shoulders. Finn also shed his before taking her hands to place it by the sides of her head. Gently, he twisted her hair around his hand, making Eirene bend her head slightly to the side, exposing her shoulder and neck. She hummed as a bolt of desire shot down to her vagina. Finn's tongue was tickling the entrance of her ear before it trailed down her neck to her shoulder. When his other hand cupped her mound, she groaned and ground herself against his fingers. She brought one arm down to cup his tight butt in an attempt to bring him closer.

"This is what the moon does."

She turned to look at him over her shoulder.

"Face the wall."

She obeyed, her eyes closed in satisfaction as Finn continued to splay kisses all over her skin.

"Finn...I want..." she moaned.

"Yes," Finn whispered and removed her tank top from the waistband of her jeans. His hot hands skimmed her ribcage and up to the underside of her breasts. Her passion flared. Eirene straightened, putting her hands to her breasts as well.

"No."

"The clasp is in front," she protested.

"I know."

Finn's open mouthed kisses across her nape and her shoulders made her breath skitter. She mewled when he bucked his stiffness against her back. She barely heard her bra clasp snap before her breasts spilled onto Finn's strong hands. His thumbs twirled over and around her hardened nipples before pinching them, causing her to cry softly. Her desire spiked. God, she was so wet. She could feel her bliss soaking her panties.

Eirene turned around in his arms to face him. He allowed it. She brought her hands to her breasts, covering Finn's hand before she rolled her fingers over her nipples. She moaned at the pleasure spike. She smiled at Finn's growl.

"Damn, Eirene, you're so hot when you do that."

A moan escaped her lips. She felt a sense of power to know that showing Finn she knew how to pleasure herself made him want her.

Finn's eyes glowed even in the dark. But it didn't scare her.

It excited her.

With a growl, he swooped down to take her mouth in a searing kiss. His tongue explored. He laid claim to her. His body scorched her. Eirene wrapped herself around him, entangling her hands in his hair as Finn held on to her waist to rub his hardness against her mound. Their tongues mated, licked, and duelled. They finally tasted each other as they were meant to do.

"You have the most beautiful tits in the world." Finn pushed her against the wall before his mouth latched on to her nipple, rubbing his lips against it and alternately sucking hard on it.

Eirene cried out and gripped his shoulders, giving small gasps of ecstasy. He lifted his head and gave the same attention to the other nipple, playing with the one he had just left, kneading it between two fingers and squeezing. Eirene's sex throbbed.

"I want you…" She was drowning in a whirlpool of desire. She grabbed at his shirt and pulled it over his head, briefly ending the kiss.

They looked at each other as they caressed one another's bodies. Their harsh breathing was the only sound in the dark hallway dimly lit by the streetlights and the headlights from passing cars. Finn took Eirene's mouth in another kiss, slanting his mouth to deepen it, and she welcomed his hot intrusion. He growled when she licked and sucked at his lower lip. Eirene splayed her hands over his chest, enjoying the feel of his taut skin rippling against her fingers. Then her hand made its way down to caress his arousal against his jeans before she cupped him.

"Oh God, so hard…" Excitement pounded inside her at the thought that soon she would feel his length in her.

Finn hissed, burying his mouth on her neck. His teeth grazed over the column of her throat. Eirene uttered a cry of delight, arching her head to give him more access to another erogenous zone. She rubbed her hand up and down his length, smiling when he groaned.

"Does that feel good?"

"Fuck, yes," he moaned.

She grabbed his head and took his mouth in a desperate kiss. Finn answered her, bruising her mouth and nipping her tongue. She brought both her hands to his butt and pulled him against her as she lifted a leg around his hip in a desperate attempt to rub her softness against his rod.

"Finn," she whispered against his mouth. "I want more. I need you."

She undid his belt, unzipped the fly of his jeans and shucked them off him. She sucked an excited breath when her hand immediately came in contact with his slightly curved, granite hard shaft. It stood at attention like a sentinel waiting for its orders.

"You don't wear anything," she murmured. Finn held his breath, watching her hand gently encircle his staff. The mere touch made it jump, and then her hand moved up and down before caressing his glans with her thumb. She saw him close his eyes and groan. His skin, so soft and pliable, held a hard treasure she wanted deep inside of her.

Finn undid her jeans. Eirene watched him as he brought them down together with her panties to pool at her feet. She looked on as Finn removed his boots and socks. He stood up gloriously naked in front of her.

"Like what you see?"

In answer, she leaned towards him, putting her hands on his chest, sighing in pleasure as her fingers trailed over his ripped pecs and torso. Then she leaned forward and flicked her tongue against his nipples, nipping, licking and sucking them.

Finn groaned in response. "Eirene Spence. You know how to bring a man to his knees. Your mouth gives me heaven." He raked his fingers through her hair, caressing her scalp. Eirene sighed against his nipple. He held her tightly by her upper arms, but she continued to lick and nip his chest down to his flat stomach.

"I want to taste you, Eirene." Finn raised her up and knelt down to take off her socks and boots.

"Oh yes." His gesture made her smile and release a sigh of delight. Finn's tongue licked his way up her legs, following the trail his hands had blazed. He gently parted her thighs when he stopped in front of her trimmed mound, inhaling deeply. He growled low in his throat. Eirene felt her face flush with desire, and when Finn placed a kiss beside her pubis, her breath caught in her throat, her teeth biting her lower lip.

Finn stood. His hard cock lightly bounced when he took Eirene's hand and led her to the thickly carpeted staircase, making her sit on the sixth step. He knelt in front of her as she leaned back. She looked at Finn with half lidded eyes. The heat in his gaze seared her, then it dropped to focus hungrily on her sex. He took her right leg and placed it on his shoulder, keeping her left one on the step. Eirene's breath came out in gasps as Finn inhaled the air around them, his shoulders and arms taut with sexual tension. He blew against her clit.

"I have never smelled anything as sweet as the honey between your thighs," he rasped.

Eirene's hips bucked softly at his words. They made her nipples pucker and her whole body ache for his touch. Anticipation caused her to lick her upper lip. "You're making me tremble, Finn."

"You asked what the moon does to me. This is what the moon does to me." He leaned forward and began kissing her mound. His mouth closed over her entire nether lips before he separated them with his tongue, licking her from slit to clit.

"Oh…!" Eirene closed her eyes and gave in to the sensual delirium. Her hips bucked at the first flick of Finn's tongue on the little bundle of nerves. Unbelievable pleasure spiked through her. Ecstasy pulsed a different beat through her core as her engorged button throbbed underneath Finn's expert lips. His tongue swirled around her, teased her, and he put his mouth over the sensitive nubbin and sucked hard. Flicks alternated with thrusts. Fast then slow. Eirene's hips lifted against his mouth, begging for more. Finn obliged her as he held her tush like a platter with her fruity clit served to him like ambrosia. Eirene's moans became rounder, and she whimpered at the graze of his slight stubble against her labia. Finn made a noise of satisfaction when Eirene cried out as his tongue delved into her delicious channel.

"Oh God, yes! More!" She whimpered.

The low rumble that came from his chest sent the vibrations through her clit. Not clearly seeing what Finn was doing to her but feeling it in every pore of her body was an incredibly erotic thing. She reached out to rake her fingers through his hair. She threw her head back once more and gasped, feeling Finn's finger slide into her core and pleasure her. The walls of her vagina clenched over Finn's finger and opened to accommodate another digit. Both fingers coaxed her, teased her, and gently hooked inside of her to reach her g-spot. Eirene felt her womb muscles tense. She was close to her climax. She reached out for it. Her pants and strangled whimpers rose in volume.

"Finn! Oh, God! This feels so good!"

Finn looked up over her mound and watched as waves upon waves of ecstasy washed over her body.

He lifted his head, his mouth glistening in the dark. "You are so, so beautiful."

He dipped his head again as he licked her sweet spot with his tongue, rubbed it with his thumb and increased the tempo of his fingers thrusting inside her. Faster and faster he went. Eirene's hips bucked, then her pleasure spiralled out of control. She jerked as she screamed her climax.

"Finn! Yes!"

Aftershocks fluttered through her sex as Finn allowed her to float down.

Eirene's heartbeat still hadn't returned to normal when Finn straightened and hovered over her. She smiled, her lips parting, knowing that Finn could see her. She sighed in satisfaction as his shaft nudged at her clit, causing her to shudder. She leaned forward and reached down, holding Finn's erection in one hand and his balls with the other. Before Finn could catch his breath, Eirene leaned forward and bent her head to take his manhood inside her mouth.

"My turn."

CHAPTER SEVEN

Finn couldn't decide which he liked more. Eirene's cries of ecstasy, her addictive sweetness which brought his taste buds to life, or the fact that she had her mouth on his cock, moaning as she sucked and licked.

He decided he liked them all.

He closed his eyes as his dick enjoyed Eirene's mouth and tongue. He had imagined what it would feel like to have her velvet lips around him, but the reality was more pleasurable than anything his imagination could conjure. His heart hammered in his chest. His ass cheeks and thighs tensed, while Eirene's mouth moved up and down his thick rod. Finn threw his head back and groaned as Eirene stroked his length, her mouth and lips closed around his balls, kissing them almost reverently.

"That's right, Eirene. Suck me."

A soft growl came from Finn's throat when Eirene hummed. The vibrations travelled through his balls and up and down his length. His hands suddenly shot up to brace themselves against the walls when Eirene lifted his sac to kiss the underside and lick his perineum. He could feel his cock tense and get ready to spill. His knees almost buckled when her mouth returned to suck him, her cheeks hollowing with her need.

Then Finn pulled her up. His jaw clenched at the flare of lust that zinged up and down his spine when her mouth made a popping sound as she let go of the sensitive head. He hissed at the passion he saw in her eyes. His body burned as his gaze raked over her body. Her kiss-ravaged mouth was parted and Finn saw that passion had plumped her lips, making them redder.

"Beautiful," he breathed. Eirene smiled before she raised up to plant a languid kiss on his mouth. Finn crushed her in his arms. His tongue plundered without permission and she opened up, returning his passion without hesitation.

Without breaking the tender melding of their lips, Finn encircled his arm around Eirene's waist and slowly brought her back to sit on the step. He knelt in front of her again and slanted his mouth to deepen the kiss before he prodded his rock hard cock into her tender opening. Eirene whimpered and lifted her hips, offering herself to him. He nudged in, opening her wider. Finn felt his shaft strain and he sighed his deep pleasure as he worked himself slowly into her hot wet channel. His eyes closed when he heard Eirene moan and purr as he pressed deeper and deeper until he was seated to the hilt. He moved his pelvis as he knelt on one knee. He withdrew and chuckled softly when Eirene whimpered, watching her face light in ecstasy when he slowly thrust back inside. Finn grunted in satisfaction at the feel of skin against skin. Shaft against welcoming channel. Groans and cries of erotic delight resounded off the walls as he stepped up the pace. He felt the werewolf part of his blood flood through him and harden his shaft even more. He thrust so far into her heat that he touched her womb.

"Finn," Eirene gasped, her eyes widening.

He stopped.

"Am I hurting you?" His voice strained with lust. Ancients! He couldn't stop now. Eirene's tight sheath was driving him crazy.

"No, don't stop," she whispered as she lifted her hand to cup his face. "You're getting thicker and longer?"

"Yes," he said, his jaw clenching. He moved to pull out.

"No, don't go. Don't leave me."

Finn groaned when she moved her pelvis forward to

take him back in. She moaned softly as he obliged, leaning up to lick his taut nipple before blazing a trail with her tongue to his neck, licking, nipping, sucking.

"More, Finn," she whispered huskily in his ear. "I want more. I want it harder. I want it deeper." Eirene lay back as her hands skimmed down his torso, holding on to his hips, squeezing and kneading them. "Please."

Finn's chest constricted with an unfamiliar emotion. The desire to please Eirene and see her happy replaced the need to simply slake his lust. There was a fissure on the wall he had built around his heart, allowing a ray of tenderness for the woman beneath him to shine through. He intensified the kiss and at the same time thrust hard into her. She cried out against his mouth, her breath harsh and staccato like. Finn moved, in and out, swivelling his pelvis against hers. Eirene lifted her hips, her head falling back in ecstasy. She made small sounds every time Finn's pelvis moved against hers with quick thrusts.

Finn looked down at Eirene's body, from her breasts and puckered nipples down to her stomach and her trimmed mound. Her entire body was flushed with the aura of intense arousal. He groaned when her channel clamped around his cock. Eirene's breasts quivered faster and faster as Finn thrust harder and deeper, eliciting deeper moans and cries from her. He leaned over to latch onto Eirene's exposed neck. He kissed and licked until he gently sucked the skin over her pulse, bringing the vein into sharp relief. He sucked hard without using his fangs.

"Yes!" Eirene turned her head giving him her neck.

The taste of her blood filled Finn's mind, exploding through his neurons.

Along with her taste came an astounding piece of knowledge.

Eirene was a Cynn Cruor mate.

The question now was whether she was his. His scent needed to be on her when a Cynn Cruor brethren smelled her. It was a scent undetectable by a purely human nose. If he marked her, she belonged to him. No other Cynn Cruor could claim her until she decided otherwise. For a woman could only be completely a warrior's mate when they came willingly and if they rejected the warrior, then the immortal would live the rest of his life without one.

The taste of her salty, sweet skin drove him wilder. He knelt on both knees as he covered Eirene's body with his. Finn held on to her hips, thrusting harder, deeper, and faster. He groaned as his balls tightened, slapping against her backside. Eirene's cries came in puffs of ecstasy until she screamed her climax. Her weeping sex throbbed and gripped Finn's manhood in a snug vice, milking him as he went in and out until he growled and finally shouted his release against Eirene's neck, calling out her name. His seed spurted into her womb, bathing and warming it. His heartbeat pounded inside his ribcage, the warmth of their coupling spreading through him like the fire in a forge. He felt Eirene's essence seep into his very marrow finally feeding the Kinaré, strengthening him like no other. Not even Zac adriserum or the essence he willingly given by other women gave him this strength. The ramifications of mating with Eirene opened wide in front of him.

He was now at her mercy.

He held himself up over Eirene with both his arms braced beside her head. He was about to withdraw from her when she placed her hands on his hips.

"Please don't go," she said softly. "Not yet."

Finn let his forehead lean against Eirene's even as she lifted her mouth for a long and sensual kiss. Eirene's arms slid over his back. By the Ancients, he loved the way her hands smoothed over his sweat-slicked skin. He felt her racing heart slowly turn to a semblance of normalcy as his own heartbeat thrummed back to a slower pace.

****

Eirene floated down from a pure cloud of bliss. Delicious shivers stroked her body when Finn kissed her forehead, then trailed kisses down her temple, making a beeline to nip at her neck. He was semi-hard inside of her and Eirene could feel another wave of lust teasing her core. She trailed her fingers over his skin and arched her back so her nipples could brush his chest. She heard the low rumble of laughter in Finn's throat as she began to run her fingertips up and down his back, then slowly caress his tight butt cheeks.

"You're as insatiable as I am."

Eirene smiled. "I never realized I was ohhh..."

Finn's right arm encircled her waist while his left arm braced his weight against the step as he pulled out of her. She sighed, her body boneless and sated. She linked her arms around his neck when Finn lifted her and carried her up the stairs. It felt so good being near Finn. She had never felt safer than she did now, in Finn's arms. She buried her face in his neck, licking and gently sucking his throat. She inhaled his scent of spice and musk and their joint sensual smell. God, his scent was making her want him again.

Finn walked towards her bedroom and to the bathroom.

"How?"

"I can see even in the dark, remember?"

Finn set her down in the bathroom before turning

on the tap for her. Eirene entered the stall, sighing as the warm water gently rained on her back, her legs wobbly after their passionate lovemaking.

"You go ahead," he said. "I'll get our clothes from downstairs."

Eirene had other things in mind.

"A kiss before you go?" She asked as her eyes seduced him. She stepped back to allow Finn to enter the stall.

Finn swooped to take her mouth in another heart stopping kiss. Fire started to swell in her belly. Eirene moulded her body against his, their tongues teasing each other. Her hands splayed over his chest, her palms overly sensitive, enjoying the play of his muscles beneath them. Finn drew a hard breath before crushing her to him. Excitement poured into the apex between her thighs when Finn's cock swelled against her stomach. His breath was harsh with need as his stubble scrapped against her neck before dipping towards her breasts. Eirene arched her back and gave a rapturous moan when his mouth captured her left nipple, twirling the tight erect bud around his tongue. Her hips nudged against him and she smiled when she heard his low growl.

She laughed softly.

"Our clothes," she whispered.

"Can wait," he muttered against her areola before he gently grazed it with his teeth.

Eirene revelled at the silky feel of his hair as she held his head about her breast. She moaned at the jolts of electricity his tongue ignited, causing her femininity to weep again. She lifted her leg against his hip and reached down between them to slide her hand up and down Finn's heated shaft. With a growl, Finn lifted her to allow her to place her legs around his waist. The warmth of the shower spray heightened the sensual atmosphere. Finn lifted her and gently backed her against the wall.

Eirene returned every hard kiss, every thrust of Finn's tongue against hers. She held him tight, urging him to take her, her gasps coming fast from her lips. Finn ended the kiss and looked at her with smouldering hunger. Eirene's eyes widened, then fell to half-mast when she felt Finn's hardness slowly sink into her again. She moaned at the pleasurable sensation of her channel readily bathing his shaft with her slick juices.

"Eirene, look at me. I want to see your eyes as I take you. I want to know how much you want me."

Eirene's eyes opened. His commanding words fed her excitement, and she did as he demanded. She looked at his eyes, turbulent with desire. The gold flecks were back in his midnight blue pupils, looking like tiny rays of the sun against a lunar eclipse. The heat of his hunger caressed her, teased her, and claimed her. She felt as though his heat had tiny tendrils which licked at her skin and teased her hardened nipples. She gasped and hummed when Finn placed his hands underneath her ass to hold her closer, his thrusts bringing her nearer to the precipice. Finn turned on the heat by pumping faster, harder, and deeper. Eirene's breath caught in her throat. She gripped his shoulders to steady herself. Her eyelids wanted to close at the sheer ecstasy of Finn's rod thrusting into her. She whimpered, then looked down. Her channel's lips felt thick and slick as it ate every inch of Finn's cock, while it appeared and disappeared into her.

"Eirene…look at me."

Her eyes snapped back to his. Her lips parted as her gasps came faster. Every slam of his pelvis against hers, every delicious friction of his shaft against her clit brought her closer to the edge. She felt herself melt at the dark desire that glowed in Finn's eyes, while his cock hammered her desire drunk sex.

As though it couldn't get any sweeter, Finn suddenly pistoned in and out of her at a much faster pace, and reaching down between them, he rubbed her clit with his thumb. The combination of delicious sensations drove her right over the edge.

Eirene's orgasm caught her unawares. Even as Finn told her to keep her eyes open, she couldn't, as her moans reached a fevered pitch and she screamed her release. Her body jerked with the strength of her climax. Finn threw his head back, groaning before he followed her over, saying her name again and again until both fell into each other's arms, limbs entangled, waiting for their hammering hearts to calm down while the shower softly rained on them.

CHAPTER EIGHT

Eirene stirred and stretched, but stopped when she felt the soreness between her legs. Her mouth slowly lifted in a soft smile. It was a delicious kind of soreness she didn't mind having. Memories of the night before and the hours of the early morning flooded her mind as her body remembered each and every delicious detail of Finn's lovemaking. Finn had been gentle with her when they'd bathed together. They had explored each other as water cascaded over them, their mouths never far apart. After going to bed, they'd made love again, Finn cradling Eirene in his arms as she drifted into an exhausted sleep.

Though the blinds were closed, the sunlight still washed the room with its warm glow. Eirene checked her mobile phone on the bedside table. It was close to noon. She groaned, and turned to Finn's side of the bed. He was gone.

Eirene sat up and swung her legs over the bed to stand up.

"Oh…" Damn, she almost couldn't walk. She tried to suppress her giggle, and shook her head when she couldn't.

Finn's jacket and shirt were thrown over the chair across the room, together with the rest of her clothes. She ran to the bathroom to sluice water on her face and swirl some Listerine in her mouth. Her gaze moved to the shower. She was never going to look at her shower in the same way again.

Walking back to her room, she opened her closet and grabbed a clean set of underwear and a white tee before slinking her legs into black jeans. She ran her brush quickly through her hair, then left the room in search of Finn. She found him pacing the lounge only in his jeans, which rode low on his hips. Eirene sucked in her breath at the sight of his lean, muscled and bronzed body. She wondered if he spent much time under the heat of the sun. Eirene swallowed as her mouth watered, wanting to lick every inch of him again. When she heard Finn chuckle before he looked at her, she knew he had read her mind again. She groaned.

He walked towards her and cupped her face to give her a kiss.

"I'd like to do the same thing to you too, sleepyhead." Finn grinned as he spoke. "Morning."

"Noon is more like it." She smiled back as she looped her arms around his neck, then her smile faltered. "Dammit, Finn, you're burning up! Did we overdo it?"

He shook his head. "I needed last night too. It's what strengthens me, especially when we had to use my gift. All the Cynn Cruors are the same. Sex is our healing balm."

"Oh." Eirene felt herself blush hotly at the way he was looking at her. "What gift did you use?"

"I cloaked our presence and our scent from the Scatha when we were in Devon's office."

"That's the second time you did that. I'm sorry." She cupped his jaw and trailed her thumb against his cheekbone.

Finn smiled as he covered her hand with his. "Don't be. Otherwise I wouldn't have known how passionate you are. You're one hell of a sexy woman, Eirene Spence."

Eirene blushed even as she could feel her sex throb at his words. His voice was so seductive, she felt she was wrapped in a cocoon of desire growing around them, and she didn't want it to end.

"If what we had last night brought back your

strength, why are you burning up?"

"The sun's up," Finn explained. "We can tolerate the sun, but it makes our blood simmer."

"Ouch," she grimaced. She understood now why Finn was agitated. Her living room wasn't exactly dark even with the blinds closed.

"We have to get you to my office. That's the darkest room in the house."

"If it's darker than this place I'll be grateful."

Eirene nodded. "Keep on going up the stairs until you reach the top. There's only one door there. Get inside. I'll be right up with some food for us," she paused. "You do eat food, don't you?"

Finn chuckled, though it came out like a grimace.

"I'm still partly human, Eirene."

"Right," she said with a sheepish grin. "Okay, off you go." She turned towards the kitchen but Finn's heated hand stopped her. She looked back at him and her heart did a two beat tap dance at the tenderness she saw in his eyes.

"Thank you."

"No problem." Eirene felt giddy.

She took the portable phone with her to the kitchen and called the Foundation's office, telling them she had an emergency she needed to attend to, and that she wouldn't be in for the next two weeks.

"Another two weeks, Eirene?" the charity officer asked.

"Yes, sorry. I just came from my doctor. He wants me to see a specialist in London," Eirene lied. Damn! Having sex with Finn made her forget she'd already said she would take two weeks off. "You'll do fine. The systems are up to date."

"Oh, sorry to hear that," the charity officer tutted. "Of course, take your time. We can always call you."

As she ended the call, she made a mental note to talk to Devon about the charity officer. She was a volunteer, for heaven's sake. It's not like she got a salary from them. Besides, she also had a reputation of being eccentric, so they shouldn't be surprised if she was off the radar for a while.

Eirene sighed. She felt a little guilty not thinking about Devon when her thoughts and her body had belonged to Finn last night.

Belonged to him. That felt and sounded right. To her at least. Would Finn feel the same way too?

Eirene rummaged through the fridge for mushrooms, butter, and eggs. She broke the eggs and started preparing a cheese and mushroom omelette.

Her body felt warm and fuzzy all over at the thought of taking care of Finn, as though it was the most natural thing in the world for her to do so. She took a deep breath. This wasn't just a one night stand. It was more.

She wanted more.

Her forehead puckered as she poured the egg mixture into the frying pan. She took out the carton of orange juice and two small glasses stacked above each other on a wooden tray. She used the turner to check the surface of the omelette before adding the cheese and mushrooms.

How could she feel this protective of him in so short a time? Surely it was just the mind blowing sex they had. Eirene never even imagined that kind of stratospheric fucking even existed. She sighed as part of the truth sunk in. All her life she had taken care of her herself. After her mother died, she was practically left to her own devices without anyone to guide her. Except for her interest in semiotics which she shared with her father, they had nothing in common. When Devon came into her life she took over caring for him until he could stand on his own two feet. He was the closest she had to a relative, but Devon was too preoccupied looking for Penny to really devote his time to caring for her. Eirene didn't blame him for that. How could she? How could she resent a parent's worry and desire to find their child and a world where cruelty and violence were fast becoming the norm?

Now Finn. His protection had made all the difference. His safe keeping seemed to make her dreary life now all worthwhile. He had gone out of his way to protect her from those weird beings, and man did they make a team! Eirene grinned as she cooked. They sure kicked ass and ground it to dust. Fighting beside Finn was exhilarating. It made her feel complete. And the mind blowing sex…shit! Sex was constantly on her mind now. She giggled. God, she was going crazy. Weird beings and sex. What a combination! Then there was the consequence of unprotected sex.

She froze from preparing the food on the plates. Oh crap.

With the amount of sex they'd had, she could definitely get pregnant. Once she brought Finn food, she was going to slip out to the pharmacy and get the morning after pill.

Twenty minutes later, she was in front of her office door. Finn immediately opened it and relieved her of the tray, placing it on the low coffee table in front of the low couch.

"You're full of surprises, Eirene."

"Really? I didn't think I was," she said, one delicate brow arched. Finn turned to the bank of computer monitors and CCTV. Eirene's face cleared. "Oh, well it's good to keep a sense of mystery."

"I realize that."

Eirene coloured at his innuendo, pleasurable shivers caressing her spine. She walked towards the computer and moved the mouse, waking up the monitors, then took the time to brew some coffee. Soon the aroma of good quality beans permeated the air. She took a mug of caffeine and placed it next to Finn's plate. Next, she went to the wall by the door to dim the lights, giving the room a soft glow.

Eirene's mouth lifted in amusement at the way Finn devoured his food. His obvious enjoyment pleased her. She wondered what it would be like to cook for him all the time. While she was contemplating domestic bliss, she saw Finn halt midway from putting another chunk of food into his mouth. He was trying to suppress a smile. Damn! Was she ever going to learn how to close her thoughts from him?

As soon as she sat down in front of the monitors, her fingers flew across the keyboard.

"What are you doing?" Finn asked between mouthfuls.

"I'm sending a virus remotely to Devon's computer," Eirene said while she continued typing. "I'm infecting it so that no one can rebuild the data. I started the process before we left when I disabled the hard drive. Now, I'm just making doubly sure." Her eyes shifted from one monitor to the other for almost half an hour before she was satisfied that her typed commands were being followed. She turned to look at Finn as she stood.

"Will you be okay here?" She asked, changing her train of thought.

Finn looked up. "Where are you going?"

"Who says I'm going anywhere?"

He arched an eyebrow. She sighed, a little exasperated.

"I have to get something."

"From where? You told me you needed to pick up something from here, that's why we didn't go straight to the Faesten."

Eirene didn't want to answer his question, but she also was uncomfortable lying to him. His direct approach made her want to squirm a little. Shutting her eyes, she concentrated on putting a barrier against him reading her mind.

"Why are you suddenly thinking of the Three Blind Mice nursery rhyme?" Finn frowned, but his eyes were alight with laughter.

"So that you won't be able to read my mind," she muttered. "I'll be right back."

Before Eirene could open the door, Finn's hand covered hers on the doorknob. Just the feel of his touch was enough to get her wet. She sucked in her breath and felt her knees almost buckle beneath her. The heat of Finn's body was wreaking havoc with hers, and she had to suppress a sigh of pleasure at his nearness. Nothing in her wildest imagination had prepared her for the reality that was Finn. He had attributes of both vampire and werewolf, yet he was also the most dynamic and sexy man she had ever met. Up until a few days ago, she would have bet her life that 'mythical' creatures such as this did not even exist. She was wrong. Even more amazing was the fact that he was also the most incredible man she had ever known. And she was sleeping with him! It was all so surreal.

"Eirene?"

"Hmmm...?"

"Is something wrong?"

"Nothing's wrong. What could be wrong?" She needed to get to the pharmacy. The sooner she got the pill the better.

"Ahh..."

Eirene's eyes snapped open.

"What's ahh?"

Instead of answering, Finn's head bent down and his mouth found hers. Eirene sighed, her body gravitating to Finn as her arms looped around his waist. Finn's hand cupped the back of her head as he angled his mouth to delve into the kiss. His tongue demanded entry to what already belonged to him. A ball of warm sweet fire blossomed inside Eirene, and she returned every kiss, welcoming his tongue's possession of her lips and mouth. He tasted of cheese and coffee. He growled softly when Eirene sucked gently on his tongue. He moved away from her lips and blazed a trail from her mouth, down the side of her throat, to the erratically beating pulse at the base of her neck. Eirene shuddered when he lifted his head to lick her earlobe.

"No matter how many times we have sex, Eirene, you won't get pregnant."

Eirene's eyes flew open. She placed her palms on his chest and pushed against him. She whimpered at the glorious feel of his taut chest against her palms, but her curiosity about his statement temporarily pushed all sensual thoughts from her mind.

"Are you...you know...?"

Finn laughed.

"Your candour is very refreshing."

Eirene lifted an eyebrow.

"And your statement is very archaic. Now spit it out. Why can't you get me pregnant?"

Finn's shoulders still shook. Finally he took a deep breath to stop himself from laughing.

"A Cynn Cruor and his mate are always equals. They have to decide together if they want to have a child. Only after that decision is made does the seed of a

Cynn become potent. And the most potent time for a Cynn is on the night of a full moon. If they don't want to have children, then it won't happen. It's always a joint decision."

"And what does this mean now that we've had sex? And please don't think I'm asking if I'm your mate." Eirene added quickly.

A dark emotion passed over his features so fast, that when it disappeared, Eirene believed it might have been just her imagination.

"You're still not going to get pregnant," he said, shrugging.

"Right." Eirene averted her eyes, but her palms remained on his chest. Damn! Touching Finn felt so good. "Night of the full moon. When is that?" She began rubbing her palms against his nipples. Her eyes smiled at the deepening desire she saw in his eyes.

"Three nights from now."

"Oh."

Finn kissed the end of her nose.

"So you have nothing to worry about."

"Uh, okay," Eirene said, drawing the last word out before her brow furrowed. She should be glad she didn't have to worry about contraception. This was after all—just sex. Mind blowing, but nonetheless it was just lust between two consenting adults. Somewhere out there was Finn's mate, who would bear his children and belong to him. And for some unknown reason, the idea of him with someone else made her wistful. She brushed the thought aside. Finn wasn't hers.

He could never be hers.

Why the hell was she thinking of that possibility?

"You're scowling."

"Huh? Oh, sorry. Just thinking of what to do." She evaded as she moved out of his arms and strode towards the computers. At least she'd been able to keep that thought from him. Maybe she was getting better at this whole thought blocking process. Eirene pinched a piece of egg and sat down beside Finn, who had returned to drink his coffee.

"Are you feeling better?"

Finn nodded. "Thanks, I can feel my blood returning to normal."

"Must be pretty uncomfortable," she said. She sipped from her mug before popping a wayward mushroom into her mouth.

"Occasional hazard." He shrugged before he pinched a piece of omelette and brought it to Eirene's mouth. Finn's grin was devastatingly sexy when her lips closed over his fingers, naughtily flicking her tongue against his fingertips. He tore a bit more for himself. Eirene felt giddy as she stared at his mouth chewing his food. It was like kissing him all over again.

He inclined his head to the computer and CCTV screens. "Was that how you realized who Roarke and I were? By going through the CCTV?" Finn stood beside her chair, his groin at Eirene's eye level.

She smiled. "No. I saw men enter my house but couldn't remember anything or what you looked like."

"But you did remember," he seemed deep in thought. "And that has never happened before. Being able to erase an innocent observer's memory has always made our work much easier."

Eirene didn't know what to say. She had no explanation why she regained her memory of him. "I didn't at first. I knew something was wrong, something was missing. I was drained, not only of my memory, but also my strength," she made a stern face at Finn. "I thought I was getting dementia."

He shook his head. "I don't know. You are

different. You were an exception." Eirene wasn't buying into that. The look on Finn's face showed that he might have an idea why she was different, but he wasn't telling. Night after night, she had dreamed about him or at least about the way he felt. Maybe they were connected in some way. Eirene shook off the notion. She didn't want to start hoping for something she couldn't have. "You depend on this ability to steal memory. It has helped you survive. What are you going to do if technology changes? You know science is making strides in every field every day."

"I don't think they'll find a way to combat our powers. To do that, they'd have to know we exist. That's not going to happen."

Eirene shrugged as she continued punching on the keyboard.

"What are you doing now?" Finn sat on the spare ergonomic chair beside her. His elbows rested on his knees as he cradled his mug in his hands.

"Devon's bastard of a client, Dac to you," she looked at him. "Refused to pay up. I always put a stop gap measure in my codes. If the other party does not live up to their end of the agreement, I freeze the last part of the program. If the deal falls apart and they already have the complete program, I destroy it. Remotely."

"Impressive."

Eirene felt giddy when Finn stared at her in admiration. Warmth heightened the colour of her cheeks.

"Too bad we'll need to look for Dac again. That's going to take another bloody long time." Finn leaned back in his chair. He held his mug in one hand as he raked his hand through his dark hair with the other.

"That's not exactly true." Eirene replied, not quite sure how much to tell him. She bent her head, her body still facing front. She knew Finn was looking at her, waiting. She worried her lower lip.

"I could nibble your lip for you if you like."

Eirene's eyes snapped to his and her heart somersaulted. She cleared her throat.

"As much as I would like that, we won't be able to catch Dac and the Scatha if we're in bed the whole day."

Finn gave her a grin that made her want to retract her statement.

"Fair enough. So what did you mean about locating Dac?"

Eirene turned her attention back to the flat screen.

"Each program I create is meant for a specific system. It fixes the glitches in the system to make sure it's secure. Until another hacking evolution ensues."

She continued typing as she spoke.

"I have a trick up my sleeve. Once the program is uploaded into the client's system, it sends a signal to my computer to let me know if the program is working. If there are problems, I send a new batch of codes to fix the system at no extra charge."

Eirene saw she had Finn's attention. He drew closer to her as he stared at the monitor in disbelief.

"Are you saying...?"

Eirene pressed the 'Enter' key. The computer brought up a map grid of the entire city of Manchester. On it was a blue blinking dot.

She smiled at him triumphantly.

"I've found Dac."

CHAPTER NINE

Finn was stunned. All this time the Cynn Cruors had been looking for Dac and the Scatha Cruor, and because of one girl, they were closer to catching Dac than ever before.

Correction.

One woman.

One intelligent and desirably hot woman.

Finn gave Eirene a hard kiss, pouring all of his joy and gratitude into it.

"Thank you." Finn stood to fish his phone from his jeans pocket. Roarke answered on the second ring.

"You better have a damn good explanation for not bringing Eirene here last night."

"We found Dac."

"No shit."

"Yes shit." Finn wasn't in the mood for Roarke's skepticism right now. Getting a team to Dac's location trumped everything else.

"How?"

"Eirene placed a tracking code on the program she made for Dac as a precautionary measure," Finn replied.

"Precautionary measure? Against what?"

"Against breach of contract." Finn said. "She does it for every client Devon sends her way. It's also her way to make sure that the program she gives them actually fixes the problem."

"You're serious?"

"I don't fool around about Dac, Roarke."

Roarke whistled. "Impressive."

"That's what I told her," Finn replied.

"He won't be able to move until later. The sun's too hot for him to leave his sanctuary, but it's also too hot for us to be able to attack."

Finn heard Roarke's frustration.

"I will get a message to the other Faestens and see if they have any Cynn mortals visiting Manchester at the moment and find out if they can spare several to help with capturing Dac. Manchester mortals are thin on the ground at the moment with the spat of child abductions."

"If we wait too long he will disappear."

"The sun's too bright, Finn. Let us know where he will be and we'll have the Cynn mortals watch the place until we get there."

"I'll go."

"How the hell are you going?" Roarke snapped in exasperation. "By the time you get to wherever the hell Dac is you'd be boiling in your own blood."

Finn exhaled loudly. He knew Roarke was right. The fact that he had to stay in Eirene's dark office drove his brother's point home. But he couldn't let Dac get away. He closed his eyes and saw the vague images of his mother and father before they had left the abbey and the sacrifice they'd made. He couldn't fail his parents.

He wouldn't.

"Let the Cynn mortals watch the place for us until the sun sets." Finn reluctantly agreed. "We'll text you the coordinates."

"We?" There was quiet curiosity in Roarke's voice.

Finn didn't bother answering Roarke's question. At the moment he couldn't answer his friend and brother because he didn't know what was happening himself. He had never felt so alive with a woman as he did with Eirene, and it was scaring him. Eirene was a critical piece of the puzzle, only *this* puzzle. They needed to find Dac and not lose the chance of ending the war between the Cruors. That was all. Afterwards Eirene would disappear from his life.

Then why did that thought bother him? Didn't he want Eirene to disappear from his existence so he could concentrate on his mission? He scowled as he tried to concentrate on what was important. He closed his eyes and thought of his parents. The need to avenge their deaths loomed large in his mind. Much better. He was now in more familiar territory.

How long had it been since his parents had died? Sometimes he became ridden with guilt when he found it difficult to remember their faces. There had been no cameras then to record their images, and whatever paintings they'd had of them as a family had been destroyed when the Scatha razed his family's home to the ground.

The Scatha had not bothered to look for him in an abbey. They spurned holy places. They had left in the middle of the night, driving their horses to exhaustion until they'd reached their destination. His parents had promised to return for him on the morrow. The morrow came and went. It became weeks, then months, until finally the friar told him his parents had died. At the age of eleven summers, he was suddenly alone in the world. Memories of the love they'd showered him with were like a fine mist that danced over his skin, yet never touching him. The loving embrace of his mother. The wise words of his father. The hurried packing and leaving his warm bed in the middle of the night. The long travel to the abbey. The tear-stained goodbyes and painful smiles of his parents as they told him he had to stay with the friar because it was too dangerous to take him with them. He had begged, screamed and cried until the huge wooden doors of the abbey had closed, and the night had swallowed his parents.

"Finn, we will get him." Roarke's voice broke through the haze of his forgotten pain. "I promise."

"Yes, we will." Finn's tone was devoid of emotion. "We'll keep tabs on Dac."

"Good. I'll check on you later. And be careful. You don't want to do anything you'll regret later. Do you understand?"

"I'm fine, Hamilton," he called his friend and leader by his last name. "What's with the sudden concern?"

"It's three days 'til the full moon, Qualtrough," Roarke retorted. "You know what that means and you're with Eirene."

Finn remained silent.

"Oh, shit. It's happened, hasn't it?"

"Later." Finn disconnected the call before returning to Eirene. He felt his blood warming, but it wasn't because of the sun's rays kept at bay by the dark red blinds. Roarke had just reminded him of what he was trying to move away from. A different kind of blood bubbling. The sweet and addictive bubbling of sex, of the pleasure and bliss of being inside Eirene. The memory of how her sex felt wrapped around his cock, how her hips gyrated against his, how it felt to sink deeper inside of her with each glorious thrust. The sensation of his essence pouring into the most beautiful cavern he had ever been fortunate enough to fill.

Finn closed his eyes and bit back a groan of longing. His dick ached and twitched at the memories his mind conjured, straining against the zipper of his jeans. But he couldn't do that to Eirene. Not yet. He had loved her hard and well. During the heat of their lovemaking, he had grown thicker and longer. Finn was afraid that Eirene was sore. He didn't want to hurt her. Finn frowned. Since when did he care about the woman he bedded as long as his cock was satisfied? But thinking of another woman other than Eirene suddenly seemed repugnant. After so many wham-bam-thank-you-ma'ams over the centuries, he usually had no compunction about leaving them, and was never bothered about keeping in touch with a previous partner.

And yet, why Eirene?

Eirene was different. Smart, sassy, spunky. And definitely sexy. Foolhardy even. Finn shook his head at the memory of her taking on three Scatha single-handedly. She could have been killed. She should have been killed. The thought brought a tightness, like a steel vice, around his chest, making it hard to inhale. He absently rubbed the area over his heart to ease the discomfort. If he hadn't been in the Park to cover their scent, she would have surely been raped or killed.

Or both.

Finn clenched his fist. Now that he had tasted her, he was finding it hard to let go. Her blood called out to him like a seductive whisper which promised him untold pleasures that only she could fulfill. Her blood sang to him, telling him Eirene was his mate.

Finn drew in a harsh breath.

"Finn, is everything alright?" He heard Eirene swivel her chair to face him. "Oh God, Devon!"

He turned to face her, finding it difficult to bank the desire that darkened his eyes, making molten flecks appear.

"No, it's not Devon." he gritted. "I'm sure Devon's fine. Zac is a brilliant doctor."

"Then what is it?"

Finn raked his hand through his hair before he placed it on his hip. Did he dare tell her? Did he dare say that he felt like the male equivalent of a bitch in heat because of his overwhelming urge to rut? In all of his immortal days he had never felt the burden of his wereblood more than he did now, and it did not subside even with the sun high in the sky.

And what about tonight? Finn sighed. If they were back in the Faesten, he'd be able to avoid her. When he did, not one of his Cynn brethren would dare touch her. That is, if they noticed his scent on Eirene. She would be strictly off limits. His brethren would have to find their release elsewhere.

Finn made his way to the low couch, near enough to Eirene, but out of her reach.

"I just feel frustrated about not being able to track Dac in this heat," he said instead.

Eirene turned back to the computer screen, checking the other monitors for activity for her other clients' computer systems.

"It doesn't look like he's going anywhere," she murmured, her profile in sharp relief against the screens' light. "Finn?"

He couldn't answer. Desire slammed him like a tidal wave. The sound of his name on her lips was enough to make him want to walk over to her, pick her up and make love to her right there on the sofa. He grunted, not trusting his voice to hide his lust.

* * * *

Eirene noticed the tension surrounding Finn from the moment he spoke with Roarke. Their voices were too soft for her to hear what they were saying, so when he finished the call, she wondered why he looked so defeated. How could he feel that way when they were so close to capturing Dac? She had never expected her life to change so drastically in just seventy-two hours. What if she hadn't gone to the Park that night? It would have been so easy to stay away. She winced as she remembered Devon's shouts still ringing in her ears. They'd had many arguments over her midnight excursions to the Park. Oh, she had always been careful, but many would think her daft and many would probably say she deserved what happened to her if she did get raped or killed. Anyone who would insist on going to that area in the dead of night was just asking for trouble. However, it was the only thing she could do when her insomnia struck and she felt caged in her own home. She just needed to get out for a while. Eirene had never understood the attraction of the night for her. Even when the darkness closed in on her, the night was her friend. She loved how the evening breeze cooled her flushed face and lulled her tense muscles to relax. It wasn't like she went to the park every evening. It was just a coincidence that on one particular night she happened upon the Scatha Cruors.

And Finn.

The memory of how it felt to have his arm around her waist as he brought her body flush against his muscled chest or how his hand held her ribcage right below the underside of her breast brought warmth to her cheeks. And how he had made love to her. Lord, it was so good. He was all strength and power. All lean muscle and sex. He made love to her with an all-consuming passion, and yet he was tender. Eirene shook her head imperceptibly.

Now, as she stared at Finn, there was an air of vulnerability about him. As if he was trying to hide something. Eirene wanted to reach out to him so she could comfort him. She wanted to help ease any pain away. She wanted to be his friend. At that moment, her heart did a triple beat making the air involuntarily whoosh out of her. Finn was more than a friend. She sucked in a longer breath as a ball of warmth curled in her belly like a contented kitten. Visions of their lovemaking the night before filled her mind. God! There was no doubt about it. Sex with Finn was the best sex of her entire life and she wanted more of it.

She wanted Finn to take her so hard and so often that she would be unable to walk.

Eirene cursed inwardly, forcing her hedonistic thoughts away. Finn needed her as a friend now and she couldn't just pounce on him and get pounded into oblivion. Damn, that was what she wanted right at this moment. This handsome paranormal man had the hots for her and she wanted nothing more than to lie down, open her legs and welcome him home.

"Finn." She needed to think of something—anything—else.

His grin slowly lit his mouth. "I like the way you say my name."

She cleared her throat and licked her lower lip. Finn narrowed his gaze, looking at her mouth. Eirene's pulse beat an erratic tattoo.

"Is Dac like you? What I mean is…does he have the same blood as the rest of you do?" She added hastily when Finn arched a brow.

Finn leaned back on the sofa. Still without a shirt, his toned abs rippled as he breathed. The solitary button on the fly of his Levi's was left unfastened and she could see the intriguing V of his hips, leading down to that delicious hard stalk of muscle and flesh which lay snugly beneath the soft denim. Just the thought of getting her hands and mouth on him again brought Eirene's arousal up a notch. For someone who hardly ventured out into the sunlight, he looked as though he had spent a lot of time under the bright orb.

"Yes and no," he said. "He was once a Cynn Cruor."

"What?" Eirene was stunned. "Explain. What happened?"

"He got greedy."

"Well, anyone can see that." She gave an unladylike snort. Finn looked at her, his eyes alight with amusement. Heat crept up her neck to her cheeks.

"Sorry."

Finn chuckled then gave a low rumble of laughter. Eirene's mouth quivered before she joined in. She felt part of Finn's tension roll away from him. His eyes crinkled at the corners and his face became more relaxed. That was a good sign even though she found it weird how she was so in sync with him. She waited for him to speak.

"There's a tapestry in every Faesten about how the Cynn Cruors came to be," he said. "It depicts how the Ancient Cynn, whom we call the Ancient Eald, was able to extract the best qualities of both vampire and werewolf DNA and blended it with human blood. The Kinaré gene. Roarke and Zac already told you that in Devon's office."

Eirene nodded, but didn't say anything as she continued to sip her coffee.

"For a very long time all the Cynn Cruors lived in harmony with mortals. We intermingled seamlessly into human society, so that no one knew of our existence. Our kind married mortals and had children with them, although the children were all male. We entered the same trades as mortals, contributed to politics, even joined the military."

"People would have noticed that your kind couldn't stay out in the sunlight or that something strange happened to you on the night of the full moon," she stated.

"As you noticed, we can stay out in the sun, but not for long and not when the sun is highest in the sky," he said, then chuckled as though reminiscing. "We made up some pretty damned excellent excuses for our occasional lapses. As long as we showed mortals how good we were at our chosen professions, no one complained. Most of us joined the armies of the countries we lived in. Others who were more eloquent became politicians. We needed to have some of our kind in high places, someone influential to make sure that if we were assigned to any mission, it wouldn't be one where we would stick out like sore thumbs."

"You could probably have become assassins."

"Which we were," Finn said. "Many trained assassins were and are Cynn Cruors."

Finn stood to get more coffee.

"Dac was a general in Caesar's army…"

Eirene gasped. "He's that old?"

Finn turned to face her, giving a lopsided grin. "He's that old."

"Oh my God."

"Well that's what he wants to be. God." Finn gave her a bemused frown. "He wants to rule over all mortals. For them to bow to him. Dac sought an audience with the Ancient Cynn and the Council of Ieldran to urge, nay, demand that the human race know of the Cynn Cruors' existence. Dac wanted humans to know that it was because of the Cynn Cruor that many wars have been won. Oftentimes the loyalty of the Cynn Cruors was compromised especially when their countries went to war against each other."

"But the Ancient Cynn and the Council didn't agree," Eirene surmised.

Finn nodded.

"Dac stormed out of the Council room in the Ancient Cynn's palace. Everyone thought that Dac only needed to blow off steam. After all, he was one of the best generals the Cynn Cruors had ever produced. But one night Dac returned to the Palace, telling the guards that the Ancient Cynn had summoned him. When he entered the Ancient Cynn's private chambers, he attacked him, hoping to kill our progenitor. Without the physical presence of the Ancient Cynn, there would be chaos. A power vacuum would arise and Dac was bent on filling that vacuum. There was no one as powerful as he was, except for the Ancient Eald."

"Was Dac successful?"

"Almost." Finn leaned forward on the sofa, his face grim. "Dac hadn't considered that the Deoré, the Ancient Cynn's beloved, would always be nearby. She was a werewolf and a warrior much like the Celt's Boudicca. I've never seen her in werewolf form. The attempted assassination was long before my time. Legend has it that she attacked Dac in her werewolf form, slashing him lengthwise. The Ancient Cynn's personal guards chased after Dac, but by that time he had disappeared. The Deoré wanted to finish him off, but she couldn't leave her beloved dying in a pool of his own blood. She turned back to her human form and fed her blood to him so he could heal. But she too had been weakened by the fight and she almost died as well."

"Why would she give him her blood?"

"The blood of the Cynn Cruor's mate is the most potent cure for any injuries a Cynn warrior receives. When a Cynn Cruor and his mate bond, they exchange blood. The mate's blood strengthens the Cynn Cruor and the Cynn's blood makes the connection to his mate strong. They will always be in sync in everything they do. They can talk to each other telepathically. A Cynn Beadurinc or warrior will always have his mate with him even when he goes to war. If they have children, the mate remains with the children and the Cynn brings a vial of his mate's blood along with him. He only needs a very small amount of the blood in the vial to heal himself, should he be injured in war. Her life giving essence heals the wounds from inside and regenerates his cells. And since they are bonded, the Beadurinc heals quickly."

"How about you? Are you bound to someone?" Her question hung between them, the answer more important than either realized.

CHAPTER TEN

God, she had asked him if he were bound to someone! As soon as the words came out of her mouth, Eirene looked down at her mug, which suddenly became very interesting. Damn! Why did she ask that question? Part of her wanted to know. Part of her was afraid of what Finn's answer might be. She wasn't naïve enough to think there was more than great sex between them. She was sure that once Dac was caught, Finn would leave and her life would return to normal. But after everything she saw and knew, how the hell could things return to normal?

"No."

Eirene lifted her head. Finn caught her gaze.

"Sorry?"

"No, Eirene. I'm not bonded," he said softly. "I haven't met my mate yet."

"Oh." Her face coloured, at a loss for a moment. "Right, well…" she tucked a thick strand of her hair behind her ear. "So, that's how the war began?"

She saw Finn hesitate before nodding.

Eirene stood up and walked towards the window. She peeked out the edge of the blinds. The sun was low on the horizon, but it still bathed everything with bright light.

"Roarke wants you to stay with us until we know Dac won't come after you."

Eirene's heart almost popped out of her chest when she heard Finn's voice just behind her, his breath close to her ear. She felt his gentle breath on the loose strands of her hair. Her back straightened at the heat emanating from him, and yet she wanted to lean back for him to hold her close. The possibility that he would soon be gone from her life after everything that had happened, brought a dull ache in her heart. She was already deep in this quagmire of longing for him to belong to her, despite knowing it was impossible. Somewhere out there was his mate. His intended. She had no business coming between them. She closed her eyes as she inhaled his scent, and filed it away in her brain. That and the memories of their one night of passion should be enough for her. Later she would pick up the pieces and move on. Her life couldn't revolve around one man. Mortal or not. At least she had conquered her mind. He wasn't picking up on her thoughts anymore. Thank God!

"Dac didn't get to see my face, Finn, so I think I'll be okay," she said. "You, on the other hand, need to get to the Faesten and do whatever you warriors do before taking down an enemy."

"Dac can see as well in the dark as any of the Cynn Cruor, Eirene. Believe me, he saw you," he repeated.

She turned around, her long hair swinging as her shoulder brushed his chest. The onrush of his hunger blasted into her, causing her breasts to swell and her nipples to pucker inside her bra. Her sex pulsed once more as blood pumped into her expectant nether lips.

"What about my things?" She glanced around her office helplessly. "I just can't leave all of them here." She turned away from him, exposing her neck. She heard Finn's sharp intake of breath.

"I'll help you pack," he said, although his voice sounded strained.

Suddenly Eirene remembered the effect of the sun on Finn's blood.

"Finn, you're too close to the window. Move back." Eirene made a mistake of putting both her palms on his naked chest. Her breath caught in her throat. She looked up at him. His eyes darkened and heated. As hot as his chest under her palms. The very air around them seemed electrified.

"Eirene." Finn's mouth was just a hair's breath away. Their breaths mingled as their sighs fuelled their need for each other. "Tell me to stop and I'll stop."

"I can't."

Someone was destined for him, her mind screamed over and over again, but it was so difficult to go against the magnetic current which attracted her to him. Blood roared in Eirene's ears. Her body came alive as if Finn's body heat became the only water which could quench her thirst. Again, her mind warned her that Finn's mate was out there, waiting for him to claim her. She closed her eyes as she ached with longing. Just for now, it begged her. Let him be hers just for now.

Just for this moment.

Eirene pushed him back gently, away from the sun's dying rays so they could make their own sun, one bright enough to eclipse the energy of that great ball of fire. She cupped his face and sighed when he turned to kiss her palm.

"So beautiful," she whispered. The tip of her tongue darted out of her mouth to lick Finn's lower lip, while she brought her other hand down to his bulging erection. Then she said, "We need to pack."

With a growl, Finn possessed her mouth. Enticing. Promising. Eirene pressed her body to his, playing with the sensitive skin on his nape, while her other hand kept moving up and down his rod.

"Later, we'll pack later," he murmured, his breathing harsh as he carried her towards the couch. "I need to taste you first."

Eirene moaned when Finn covered her body with his. She could feel her vagina begin to prepare itself for Finn. It was as if she were to be a banquet for his pleasure. Finn quickly unbuttoned her jeans and she helped him take them and her panties off. There was an almost feral gleam in his eyes as they feasted on her glistening lips. He looked at Eirene. Her breathing was quick and fast.

Then he dove right into her mound.

Eirene's hips bucked as she gave a strangled moan the moment Finn speared her with his tongue.

"Finn! More, please more!"

Finn's hunger for her was voracious, and nothing else existed for her but this man and this moment. She mewled her approval when he delved into her heat and lapped the cream flowing from her. When his lips latched on to her sweet spot and his tongue duelled with it, she whimpered some more, combing her hands through his hair while she ground herself against his mouth.

Eirene arched her back, writhing underneath Finn's mouth. She moaned, fire flowing deliciously through her veins when he hummed his satisfaction against her nub. Sweet angels! She'd never been pleasured the way Finn pleasured her. Her gasps became fast pants when Finn spread her wider, giving a sexy growl as he lifted her hips to gain more access to her sex, and he thrust deeper, tongue pleasuring her over and over again. Eirene whimpered, holding Finn's head to anchor herself as her hips moved up and down against his mouth. They moved in tandem. His mouth and tongue. Her hips and clit. Finn inserted two fingers inside her and pushed inside hard and fast. A new wave of ecstasy hit Eirene, doubling the spiralling tension inside her. She was breathing hard, her cries increasing in pitch until she screamed. Finn's growl against her sex made her orgasm all the more exquisite. Tremors washed over her as Finn lapped slowly over and around her sex, bringing her down, until Eirene slowly drifted back to reality. Finn straightened up, a satisfied smile on his face. Eirene giggled when he took a napkin from the tray to wipe his mouth.

"Now that was good." Finn's eyes were still dark with desire. He moved to cradle her to his side before he kissed her. Eirene could taste her essence against his tongue. It was highly erotic. She unzipped Finn's jeans and sighed in contentment as her hand closed around him. Then she started to stroke his manhood up and down. His hips bucked against her hand as he groaned against her mouth. She felt Finn spread her legs.

"What are you doing? Ohh..." Her voice was still husky from her climax. Finn's fingers opened her nether lips before languidly playing with her clit and dipping his finger into her honey pot, while his thumb circled her clit again.

"Like it?" Finn's voice, deep with huskiness, sent shivers down her body, adding to the liquid heat between her thighs.

"Oh, yes," she sighed.

"Remove your T-shirt," he commanded.

Eirene sat up and did as she was told. Finn flicked the hooks of her bra from behind and slowly pulled the straps down her shoulders. Eirene moaned at the feel of his mouth against her shoulder.

"Now..." His voice was low and deep. "Time for dessert."

Eirene giggled until her laughter turned to cries of sensual delight.

* * * *

Sated and spent after their loft interlude, he and Eirene started packing her computers and monitors into boxes in less time than it took Eirene to pack some clothes. Blake had arrived in one of the Cynn Cruor's black Range Rovers with specially tinted windows. When he got out of the car and into the cooler confines of the house, his eyes widened, giving Finn a stunned look. Finn remained tight-lipped.

"Holy shit," Blake said as he exhaled. "Seriously?"

"Shut up," Finn muttered under his breath.

Blake recovered in a heartbeat and nodded. He and Finn quickly stacked Eirene's things and boxes, but not as fast as they would normally do. Eirene switched on the alarm before she locked the house.

Hardly anyone spoke during the drive to the Faesten, except for Eirene asking if both of them were okay with the sun still out. Blake replied for Finn, nodding and giving her a smile through the mirror.

"The special tinted glass helps a lot," Finn replied after. "It takes out a lot of the ultraviolet rays but it still feels a little uncomfortable."

The Faesten was an entire building among the other old brick buildings in Manchester City Centre. Blake maneuvered the SUV through the narrow entrance of the underground parking. As soon as the dark enclosed them, both Cynn Cruors breathed a sigh of relief. They all alighted, with Eirene carrying her rucksack. Blake dragged the pushcart parked by the elevator towards the back of the vehicle. Finn helped him stack Eirene's things on it before they entered the lift.

The elevator pinged and opened on the main lobby. Roarke and Graeme were already there, waiting for them. Finn turned to Eirene who looked awestruck. He wanted to smile at her, to put his finger under her chin so that he could close her gaping mouth, but he couldn't.

You can't or you won't? His mind taunted.

"I have to attend to a few things," he said to her.

"I'll see you later."

"Okay," she said softly, looking at him with a bemused frown.

He left her. Finn knew he was going to end up being an asshole again. He needed to think. He could feel the puzzled and angry stares of his fellow Cynn at his back.

"I'll take your computer gear to the nerve centre." Finn heard Blake say. "Once you've settled, you can come over and tell me what you want to do."

"Let me take you to see Devon first, then I'll take you to the guest room," Finn heard Roarke say as he climbed the staircase that would lead to his quarters.

Now, as he stood inside his shower stall, Finn let the water cascade all over him while he braced both arms against the wall. He shivered against the nearly freezing water yet remained underneath the spray. It was a huge contrast to the arousing heat which was now a constant in his veins.

And his insatiable desire for Eirene.

Finn closed his eyes. Each and every climax he elicited from Eirene was so erotic it brought a tingling satisfaction down his spine. Bringing her pleasure always made his hard cock even harder, to the point where pleasure and pain were indistinguishable. It was an exquisite pain he'd never in his entire immortal life experienced with another woman. The addictive sensation rivalled even the pleasure he found in his own release, which, with Eirene, brought him complete and utter bliss.

As the water beat down on him, Finn had an epiphany. A sense of destiny engulfed him. He realized something had changed. He had changed. For the first time, he was filled with a sense of tenderness and peace. The peace came from knowing there was someone who cherished him, who cared for him, who would be there for him. Would she be willing to stay with him?

He had tasted Eirene's blood. He knew the truth. Could he allow her into his life? What about his mission of hunting down Dac and killing him? Was there a way he could continue with his objective and still have a life with Eirene? She could still refuse him. Finn didn't know whether her rejection would solve his problem or destroy him. The hollow pain in the centre of his chest returned. Did it matter to him if she didn't stay? These emotions, which ran riot through him, were so alien to him that he was at a loss at what to do. He seemed to have lost all common sense. His mouth curved in an ironic smile. He could take the Scatha anytime, unscathed. One moment with Eirene and he was unravelling. She gave him peace, and deep inside he knew it was something he longed for. Not one of the women he'd had sex with in the past had ever given him this sense of solitude.

Why her?

Why Eirene?

No. It wasn't possible. Not now.

He couldn't just leave her. Not again, when he had just made love to her.

Finn had always prided himself in not getting too involved with a mortal. He didn't want to be tied down. He had a mission to help eradicate the Scatha Cruor, and to have a woman by his side would split his concentration. Somehow being with Eirene just felt right, and he was now beginning to wonder what it would be like to have a woman next to him, not to hold him down, but to be his strength and to fight beside him.

Eirene or his mission.

That was the question.

He was so damned confused.

The last few moments he'd had with Eirene in her loft office had been some of the best he'd ever known. He had worshiped her body with his mouth, and she had figuratively brought him to his knees when she had turned the tables and worshiped his cock with such tenderness. The memory of her lips around his granite hard shaft, tight against his thickness as she sucked him, made him groan.

"Eirene," he whispered, remembering what it had been like to eat and drink his fill of her. Her touch was like no other woman on earth. Finn stroked himself as memories of how her hands had expertly moved up and down his length until he'd climaxed returned to him, and how she had swallowed every bit of his essence, milking him until he had nothing left. He laid his forehead against the cold dark blue tiles. His shaft throbbed and ached to be buried deep within his lover's warm, wet body.

"Damn it, haven't you had enough?" he growled at his dick, struggling to force the erotic thoughts away. As soon as they had entered the Faesten's lobby, everyone seemed to know something had happened to them. His scent on Eirene should have been washed away by the last shower she'd taken before they had left her house. His scent would not have stayed on any other woman after sex. His scent would only remain on a woman for one reason. If she was a Cynn Cruor mate.

And Eirene was his mate.

Blake and Roarke knew. Now Graeme did and soon Zac would as well. Strictly speaking, he'd be the first among them to find a mate. Roarke had lost his beloved during the Scatha Cruors' siege of his home. Now that there was a Cynn Cruor mate in their midst, things in the Faesten would change. Every Cynn Cruor mate had the protection of all Cynn Cruor warriors, whether they were from their own Faesten or from other Cynn Cruor bailiwicks.

They would all protect Eirene with their lives.

A well of unfamiliar tenderness warmed the parts of his heart where the wall he had erected had now cracked and crumbled. After three hundred years, he had found his mate, although finding her did not necessarily mean she would be his. Eirene had to come to him willingly. He couldn't force her, nor use his gift to manipulate her mind to make her say what needed to be said. Asking to be his mate had to come from her heart. If she didn't ask, then even as a Cynn Cruor, he would live the rest of his life without her.

And that would mean a long damned immortal existence.

Finn lifted his head to let the spray gently beat down on his face. Sexual attraction, no matter how strong, would wane in time. Would it wane with Eirene? Even as his mate? All he knew was that she had already gotten under his skin. Every time he saw her, he wanted to take her in his arms and make passionate love to her. He always wanted to be near her, to be there for her, to protect her. His mouth curved into a grin. Eirene would suffocate if he was too protective. He would need to give her space.

Why the hell was he thinking of Eirene as though she was already a permanent part of his life? He closed his eyes as he sighed. The fact was he just couldn't see himself staying away. Even now, when he was in his quarters and she was in the other wing of the Faesten, he longed to be with her.

Would she want to be with him?

Finn walked back to his room, a towel around his hips. He halted mid-stride when he saw a Cynn Cruor warrior already inside his room, and leaning against the door. Roarke had a bland look on his face. "You sure took off in a hurry."

Finn ignored him. "Has she settled in?" He ran a towel through his hair before flinging it on an armchair nearby. He grabbed his jeans and pulled them on, then took a midnight blue linen shirt from the top drawer of his dresser.

"Not quite. She's with Devon at the moment. I will ask Graeme to pick her up later from her room. Both he and Blake are setting up her computer and CCTV in the nerve centre," Roarke said, leaning against the bedroom door.

A wave of pure jealousy threatened to drown Finn, so powerful that he grunted at the onslaught. His fingers dug into the wooden top of the drawers until it splintered.

"Graeme is the security expert among us, Finn." Roarke said as he pushed away from the door, his stance relaxed, but careful. "Nothing is going to happen to Eirene."

Finn nodded as he exhaled. "I know," he paused as he finished dressing. "No one told me it was going to be this difficult and quick."

"No one knew it would be." Roarke's eyes held sympathy for his brother and friend. "Finding one's mate is a unique journey for everyone. I doubt if it's ever the same."

"So I just have to grin and bear it."

"I think you're finding it difficult because it's so close to the full moon." Roarke placed a hand on Finn's shoulder. "I don't envy you. Concentrating on Dac might help get you through."

Finn closed his eyes for a moment before he sighed and nodded.

"How do you do it, Roarke?" The question was out

before he could stop it.

Pain slashed across Roarke's face.

"Shit! Sorry.... I didn't mean to—"

"It's okay, Finn. It was a long time ago." Roarke's mouth slightly lifted in a tight smile. "And why haven't I died yet? I haven't the foggiest."

Finn's smile was quick and rueful. He sat down on the chair to put on socks and tie his boots.

"Finn?"

"Yes?"

"Does she know?"

Finn's fingers paused in the midst of tying the bootlace, as if he was making a decision, then completed the task. He stood up and looked straight at Roarke. For once he allowed Roarke to see how vulnerable he was.

"No, she doesn't," he answered. "She needs to find out for herself." He took his dagger and gun before speaking. "Let's go. We've got Scatha to kill."

CHAPTER ELEVEN

From the way Finn and the others had described the Faesten, Eirene had assumed it was in the outskirts of the city. She hadn't expected it to be right dead centre of town. When the elevator opened into the Faesten's lobby, she thought she'd been transported to a world class hotel.

The Faesten was an eclectic mixture of old and new, of polished marble floors and staircases with black iron balustrades that led to the second floor.

The marble floor shone in the dim light. From the wall, scones hung on each of the four columns which supported the high dome shaped ceiling. In the centre of the floor was a huge mandala design with the words *Cynn Cruor* around the symbol. Facing Eirene was a grand staircase leading to the upper floor. Two similar, but smaller staircases flanked the main one so that anybody coming from the upper hallways did not have to use the central staircase. Underneath the right stairwell was a glass panelled wall and a door leading to the kitchen, which was done in warm tones of brown and slate. It had wood parquet floors, maple wood cupboards, slate granite counter tops, and a brushed aluminium oven and fridge. Set against the specially tinted bay windows overlooking the city centre was the breakfast nook.

Eirene looked to the left. There was a huge door with an electronic lock which could only be opened by an authorized thumb print. Behind the main staircase was a set of double glass doors that led to the library and command centre.

Roarke had met them, and as soon as he appeared, Finn told her he had things to attend to. Just like that, he was gone. Eirene felt bereft, and for a moment she felt vulnerable surrounded by all the men. They were acting a bit odd. Blake appeared to be more reserved than when she's first met him in Devon's office. And Graeme had not been able to hide his surprise at Finn's abrupt departure. He had immediately wiped the stunned expression from his face not realizing that she had noticed. Eirene had tried not to follow him with her eyes, but she had been unable to help herself. Finn had acted the strangest of all. He had almost flown up the staircase as if the devil himself were on his heels.

As though he couldn't wait to get away from her.

"I'll take you to Devon." Roarke had said, giving her a welcoming smile. "As Blake is taking your computer gear to the command centre, Graeme can bring the rest of your personal belongings to your room. I'll take you there later."

Eirene thanked Graeme as she gave her rucksack to him. Graeme gave her a wolfish, but friendly grin before bounding up the staircase, while Blake continued towards one of the massive doors in the underneath the staircase. She trailed behind, trying to take in everything around her. Eventually, she noticed Roarke waiting for her several feet away. She hurried towards him. He exuded power and virility from his broad shoulders, tapered waist, and muscular legs, but he wasn't Finn. Despite their similarities in the way they carried themselves, it was Finn who made her pulse flutter, her sex pool, and her body ache with longing. The way he always looked at her with a mixture of desire and tenderness. Of possession and freedom. Of promises and honour.

Of love.

Eirene stopped, a small surge of hope in her belly. Could it be possible that Finn felt something more? She flung the silly thought aside. Finn could never love her.

His kind dictated that he be mated and she had to, no, must accept that. How the hell could he fall for her in such a short span of time?

Even if she loved him.

Holy shit.

She swallowed hard, finding it suddenly difficult to breathe. No. This was just sex, lust, a fuck. She shouldn't interchange lust with love. Besides, she couldn't love Finn because he belonged to someone else. Someone of their kind, not a mere human like her. And the sooner her heart accepted that fact, the better it was for her.

There was no time to dwell on hopeless dreams and fantasies. She had to find out how Devon was doing. Next, she had to help the Cynn Cruors get Dac. Then she had to continue to try to find Devon's daughter, Penny. Only then would she be free to think of herself. Eirene wasn't a believer of love at first sight. More lust at first touch. She had to admit, though, that she felt empty when Finn wasn't around. But that didn't mean she was in love with him.

Roarke led her to a long oak panelled corridor which glowed softly from the sconce lights on the wall. To her left was the tapestry Finn had mentioned. Encased in non-glare glass, Eirene saw the figures of the Ancient Cynn and his Deoré during the battle with Dac and how it created the schism between the Cynn and Scatha. The figures were meticulously woven into what looked like very old cloth. It was a masterpiece of embroidery, done in a profusion of red, brown, black, cream, and blue. The scene drew her to it, riveted by the drama unfolding from the fine stitches made by expert hands. Since Finn had told her the story, the characters became so real that she kept expecting them to move and jump out of the tapestry.

Eirene didn't realize she had stopped in the middle of the corridor until she heard Roarke retrace his steps.

"Sorry," she said, giving him a nervous smile as she blushed. "I've never seen anything quite like it. It just looks so similar to the Bayeux Tapestry, but much more detailed and refined. It's beautiful. Finn told me about it."

Roarke grinned.

"Yes it is," he said. "I often come here to remind myself of who we are and the need to keep to ourselves, while at the same time being part of humanity."

"Hmmm. But you're still partly human."

"True. But we're not quite either, are we?"

"Roarke," Eirene said as she stepped beside him and lightly touched his arm. "Please don't get angry at Finn. I was curious."

He smiled. "You had every right to know. C'mon. Devon's waiting."

She had every right to know? What did he mean? They reached the end of the hallway. A stained glass window threw its colours on the floor as the sunlight's dying rays shone through. Roarke stopped in front of a polished oak door to his right. He knocked before entering.

Devon rested on several pillows propped against the headboard of the massive canopied bed. The room looked more like a very expensive and opulent hotel room, complete with burgundy brocade curtains and deep brown stuffed armchairs flanking the bed. There was an electric fireplace opposite the bed, which was unlit. Zac sat on one of the armchairs facing Devon when they arrived. Eirene saw Zac's eyes widen momentarily before whatever emotion that flashed disappeared. She looked at Roarke beside her, but his face was inscrutable.

What is going on? Do I smell horrible? Do I have drool on the side of my mouth? Eirene wondered. Why wouldn't she have drool? She was surrounded by hunky sexy men! Surreptitiously, she bowed to swipe her hand across her lips, just to be on the safe side.

Zac walked towards her with an inviting smile.

"Hey, Eirene. Welcome to our humble abode."

She raised an eyebrow.

"You're kidding, right?"

Zac chuckled. "I'll leave you with Devon."

When the two left, Eirene moved to Devon and sat on the edge of his bed. She fought the tears which threatened to spill. She had to swallow hard several times when she saw the lacerations to his face and arms, crisscrossing his skin.

"This is the second time you've seen me in a horrible state, my dear." Devon said and winced as he tried to smile. "We should stop doing this."

Eirene tried to laugh, but the sound stuck in her throat. She couldn't prevent her tears from falling. She placed her head on Devon's chest as sobs engulfed her.

"Oh, Eirene." Devon tsked, then chuckled. "It's not too bad. It just looks like it. I've had worse when I was on the streets."

"I'm sorry."

Devon frowned.

"For what?"

"For trashing your office."

Devon's chest jiggled as he chortled.

"I didn't like the interior design anyway."

Eirene sat up and laughed softly, her eyelashes spiked with tears.

"Yeah, you'll need a new office now," she said, sniffing. "Those bastards know where you work."

"Zac said I could make my temporary office here

while my wounds heal."

"That's a good idea," she nodded, squeezing his hand. "I've corrupted your office computer's hard drive and transferred the files to the cloud drive. We just have to inform the insurance company. The Cynn believe that Dac will try to find and hurt us."

"The Cynn Cruors." Devon let his head fall on the pillow as he sighed. "Who would have thought? They don't look any different from us."

"You know who they are?"

He nodded. "Zac was kind enough to let me in on their secret. I didn't believe it at first and I still find it hard to believe that they're really who they say they are. Honestly, I'd rather cast my lot with them than with the scumbags in had to deal with in the streets. Neither was it easy for him to trust me."

"Yeah, because you're a solicitor."

They both laughed with Devon wincing again.

"Why would Dac Valerian want to do that to us?" he asked, shifting gingerly to a more comfortable position. "He's got the program and he didn't pay, so the egg's on our faces."

Eirene scratched the back of her neck as she gave a rueful smile.

"What did you do, young lady?"

"Included a code that would corrupt the program I made if the deal fell through."

"You clever girl." Devon said. His eyes danced with merriment before he sobered. "You said you corrupted the computer's drive in the office."

"Don't worry. Everything's up in the cloud. Including your file on Penny."

Devon closed his eyes. He suddenly looked tired, his mouth pinched.

"Thank you."

"We will find her, Devon. No matter how long it takes." Eirene promised as she took his pudgy hand in hers, squeezing it reassuringly.

"It's been years, Eirene. Years since Janice took her away from me. They couldn't just have disappeared."

"And they haven't," she said with more conviction than she felt. "Look, you have to get well so that we can go through your file again. We might have missed something we didn't think was important before."

"You're probably right."

"Of course I am." Eirene scoffed with amusement. "I'll be back tomorrow."

As she closed the door to Devon's room, she worried her lower lip. She needed to check Devon's file on Penny. Anxiety pressed down on her mind as she wondered what could have possibly happened to his daughter.

"If there was a wall in front of you, you would have hit it already," a dry voice said a few feet away from her.

Eirene whipped her head up, the frown of concentration replaced by slight surprise.

"Sorry, I didn't realize you were waiting." She offered Roarke a half smile.

Roarke shrugged. "No problem. Come, I'll show you to your room."

"Where's Finn?" Eirene blurted before she could stop herself. If Roarke noticed her overzealous desire to see Finn, he didn't show it.

"He'll meet us in the nerve centre later." Roarke didn't elaborate any further.

They continued walking along the carpeted corridor before Roarke veered to the right where he stopped midway through.

"This is your room." Roarke said, then opened the

door and flicked the light switch on. He stepped aside for Eirene to precede him.

Eirene gasped. The room was as big, if not bigger than the entire ground floor of her house. A king-sized sleigh bed made of oak dominated the left wall and was flanked on both sides by curtained windows. An unlit marble fireplace was set on the opposite wall. Between the bed and the fireplace was the largest Turkish rug Eirene had ever seen. The design and colours of mahogany, red, dusty red, light brown, brown, and navy brought a wealth of old world charm to the more contemporary design of the room. Eirene walked further into the area facing the bed. A huge overstuffed leather armchair sat on the left hand corner with a floor lamp set snug beside it. Another door to her right led to the bathroom which from Eirene's vantage point looked almost as big as the bedroom. To the left of the bedroom door was an 18th century wardrobe made of the same dark oak as the bed.

"Do you like it?"

Eirene swung around.

"Are you kidding me?" Eirene's eyes were round as saucers. "This room is so eclectically beautiful! Are you sure this is the guest room? I mean, I'm just staying here for a while."

"It's your room for as long as you like."

"Thank you."

Roarke arched a brow before his eyes crinkled in understanding.

"I can see what Finn saw in you. You have no guile at all."

Eirene felt heat rush up her cheeks.

"And that's a good thing?" Her voice sounded small even to her.

Roarke grinned.

"You say what's in your heart, Eirene. You don't like to deceive people and neither do you like deception."

It was Eirene's turn to arch her brow as she cocked her head to one side.

"And you got all that from my saying thank you."

"Let's just say I know people." Roarke nodded. "I have to get back. Why don't you freshen up and I'll ask Zac to come and get you later."

Eirene wanted to find out why Finn couldn't be the one to get her, but Roarke had already turned to the door. With another short smile, he closed the door after him.

She sighed as she walked to the switch to dim the lights. She didn't want to freshen up. She wanted Finn. Where was he? Why had he left as soon as they'd entered the Faesten? It was only two more nights before the full moon. Was he checking on whether his mate had been found? Sadness and a tinge of jealousy sliced through her. She always knew that what she had with Finn wouldn't last. Didn't she tell herself being with him was worth it? She had grabbed onto a little bit of temporary heaven and said to hell with the consequences.

Eirene sighed suddenly, feeling drained. What a mess she had gotten herself into. Maybe Roarke was right. She should freshen up. She'd take a long shower, even though she had taken one earlier with Finn. Man, she was such a sucker for men she couldn't have. Perhaps the shower would wash away the growing pain in her heart. Hopefully she'd be able to remove the memory of Finn's hands as they touched her, his mouth as he kissed her, and his beautiful manhood as it thrust inside of her. That way she'd finally be able to concentrate on what had to be done to find Dac. Then she'd leave the Faesten with Devon. Once back at home, she'd be able to take stock of things, and in time she'd forget Finn.

Like right, who was she kidding?

CHAPTER TWELVE

Eirene had just switched off the shower when she heard a knock on the door. Hurriedly shrugging into the waffled textured robe and tying it around her waist, she wrapped her damp hair in a towel. The knock came again.

"Just a sec!"

Giving her hair a quick rub, she strode to the door. As she turned the doorknob, she looked back to make sure the towel landed on the bed.

"I thought I had an hour—Finn!"

Finn's arm was braced against the doorjamb and he had that dark look in his gaze, telling her he wanted to seduce her.

Eirene's pulse fluttered. Damn it! How this man was wreaking havoc on her body. An urgent and primal need hit her. Her breathing quickened and she had to hold on to the door to keep herself from melting at his feet.

As Finn walked into the room, Eirene let go of the door and stepped back. Finn closed it behind them, locking it.

Her heart collided against her ribs. Excitement pooled between her thighs.

But enough was enough. Maybe.

"I couldn't stay away, Eirene." Finn said, his voice husky as he cupped her face in both hands. Eirene closed her eyes at the sensual touch of his thumb on her lower lip. She moaned into his mouth when he took her lips in a searing kiss.

She too, would never be able to stay away. Even as her tongue duelled with his, desperation made her heart ache. God! She didn't have the strength to move away.

She moulded her body to his as her arms encircled his neck, caressing his nape. Finn groaned as he slanted his mouth against hers, pulling her tighter to him. Their heavy breathing was the only sound in the room. Finn lifted her in his arms and carried her to the bed, laying her down and immediately covered her body with his. She whimpered when Finn's denim encased bulge grazed her femininity. Eirene pulled the end of his shirt from his jean's waistband and sighed as her hands came in contact with Finn's flesh. With trembling fingers she unbuttoned his shirt while he untied her robe. Their mouths and tongues continued their mating ritual which fanned the flames between them. There was a desperate urgency in their movements, this need to feel skin against skin.

Finn broke the kiss to hungrily gaze at her naked body. Her nipples stood at attention just by his mere regard. When he knelt between her thighs, Eirene sighed as his callused palms moved across her belly and down her thighs and calves. He then reversed the process and brought his hands up to cup her breasts. Eirene's body arched, her head thrown back, writhing under his touch. Finn's thumbs made the peaks harder and slightly painful, but she loved every minute of it. Desire sizzled down her spine and added to the moistness of her sex when Finn bent to suckle one hard peak. She cried out softly as she held his head to keep him there. When he latched on to the other nipple, his hand reached down between them to part her folds and find her wet clit.

"Finn," Eirene breathed, her hips bucking against his hand. "Yes!"

Sheer delight suffused her as Finn inserted two fingers into her channel and worked them back and forth inside her. Eirene felt the pressure build, dragging her into a spiral of ecstasy. His fingers expertly stoked the ache deep within her. Her whimpers increased in frequency and pitch. Finn kissed her hard and Eirene raked her fingers through his hair, enjoying the feel of its smooth texture. Then she wrenched her mouth away as she exploded. She held on to Finn, allowing herself to drown in the whirlpool of passion. Her hand trailed down his arm to the fingers that still pleasured her, holding onto his hand as she continued to ride them.

* * * *

Eirene's face was lit with her afterglow. Her body flushed with the force of her climax.

Finn had never seen a more beautiful sight.

And she was his mate.

Finn propped his head on his hand and continued to gaze at the woman beside him, waiting for her breathing to calm down. He gently rubbed her pleasure nub one last time before he removed his fingers from her core.

Eirene moaned and sighed. She turned to look at him, her eyes still dark with passion. A beautiful blush stained her cheeks as she watched him put his soaked fingers into his mouth and suck. Finn closed his eyes, savouring her taste.

He gathered her into his arms, cradling her to his side. His breath hitched when he felt Eirene's hand unbutton his jeans and unzip his fly. He groaned when she took his cock in her hand and massaged it till it was hard as steel. His heart hammered loudly in his ears. He growled softly when she used her other hand to lift his shirt away from his chest and moved in to begin a wet trail from the middle of his rock hard abdomen towards his nipple. Her tongue swirled around his aroused bud before sucking hard.

"Eirene," he breathed, while his hands continued to skim her silky skin. Her wicked tongue sent bolts of lust down his shaft, making it twitch. Ancients! He needed her hot haven around his cock. He wanted her velvet heat encasing him, her inner muscles milking him. He ached to consume her and take her to heights like neither had known before.

He needed to talk to her, to tell her she was his mate and how much he loved her. He wanted to tell her he understood if she felt it was too soon. He'd ask her to see where this relationship took them. What happened next would be up to her.

"Eirene, wait."

He pushed her away firmly, but gently. Raw hurt flashed in her eyes, but she acquiesced. Finn was determined to focus on the need to tell her who she was for him, and not to give in and make love to her to ease her doubt. She sat back with her legs folded underneath her, pulling the robe around her to hide her nakedness from his eyes. Finn sat up and zipped the fly of his jeans leaving the waist unbuttoned, much to his dick's painful consternation. He curbed his desire to run his hands through her damp hair that fell in thick tendrils around her shoulders, framing her face. He watched as she got up and stood beside the bed.

"We have to talk," he said, raking his hands through his thick black hair.

She stared at him, her face pale. Anguish filled her eyes, but she held her ground. Finn could not bear it. He was about to explain when she beat him to the punch.

"You've found your mate," she said in a flat tone. Her arms were clasped around her waist.

Relief surged through Finn. It wasn't going to be difficult at all.

He grinned.

"Yes."

* * * *

The relief in Finn's voice hit her like a ton of bricks. This was it. Eirene felt her heart break. The smile on his face lit up his features. He was so handsome. So happy. Eirene felt her heart wither inside her chest. She felt lightheaded and had to blink several times to stave off the dizziness.

"Eirene. Are you alright?"

She watched Finn move across the bed towards her, and she couldn't take it. Eirene bowed her head.

Oh, God! How could he be so cruel? Did he really have to come to her room, pleasure her to oblivion only to tell her afterwards he had found his mate? Why couldn't he just go and allow her to lick her wounds in peace? Why couldn't he just stay away for the time she was here until she could leave?

"I'm really happy you found her Finn," she said, trying to smile. "Now you'll have to excuse me so I can get dressed. We need to catch Dac, remember?"

Knowing Finn was lightning fast, she sprinted to the bathroom, slammed the door, and locked it behind her.

"Eirene…"

She sank down on the floor. The tears finally fell in torrents. She sobbed out her pain. Her heartache burgeoned to fill her entire chest. She felt like she was suffocating and had to drag air into her starved lungs. It seemed her windpipe had suddenly become too narrow. Damn it! If this was just a fling, why the hell was it so painful? She felt as though her gut had been wrenched and twisted inside her. The pain in her heart was becoming unbearable.

How could she have fallen for Finn so quickly?

"Eirene!"

She crawled away from the door and made her way

to the cream wicker chair by the bathroom's stained glass window. She sat and curled inside the seat, trying to make herself as small as she felt. Hugging her knees to her chest, she jerked every time she heard Finn banging on the door. He kept calling out her name, while she sobbed her grief.

"Eirene, open up! We have to talk."

"Go away, Finn! Leave me alone," she muttered in between hiccups. She took a deep breath. "We'll talk later."

"Damn it!"

Eirene squealed when the door flew off its hinges, crashing to the floor. She scrambled to her feet.

"Go away!"

"Not until I talk to you." Finn growled, frowning at her tears. He stood a few feet away from her, looking like an avenging god.

And her sex throbbed and wept at the sight.

"I don't want to talk."

"If you gave me a chance to speak—"

"What else is there to say?" She flung back. "You have found your mate."

"I love you."

She gave an almost hysterical laugh, the tears still spilling down her cheeks. Finn loved her. Oh, God! How much more pain did she still have to bear?

"Please, don't say that."

"Why the hell not?" Finn's tone of voice was harsh and angry.

"I have no intention of being your mistress."

"Mistress? What the bloody hell are you talking about?"

"I don't think your mate will approve of you loving someone else. So please, go. The rest of the Cynn Cruors are waiting."

"Oh, bloody hell, Eirene!"

Before she could react, Finn hauled her in a fireman's carry. She squealed as he dumped her on the bed. She tried to move away, but Finn pinned her underneath him.

"Stop it, Finn, get off!" Eirene sucked in her breath as her robe parted, exposing one breast. She saw Finn look down and growl softly, but he didn't do anything.

"Not until you listen to what I have to say."

"The Cynn—"

"Have been told to start without us."

"They don't know the coordinates," she retorted.

"I gave it to Graeme. He's our expert. He'll know what to do."

Eirene laid her head back in resignation. Her heart continued to flutter with Finn on top of her, but also throbbed with the pain of losing him. What a complicated muscle. She bit her lower lip to stop from moaning when she felt his arousal nestled against her pelvis.

Her body was such a traitor.

"When I met you, I never thought I could fall for you so hard in such a short span of time. I want you so much. I love you, Finn Qualtrough, with all my heart," she solemnly touched his face in a gentle caress. "I love you so much, it hurts to be happy for you when I know you can never be mine."

Finn frowned before he sighed and closed his eyes. "Eirene, I --"

She placed a finger over his lips. "Let me have one last time with you, and then I'll let you go to your mate. Learn to love her, Finn. Forget me."

Finn's eyes darkened at her admission. She felt a slight tremor run through him before moved her finger out of the way and leaned over to kiss her, demanding that she open up for him. He slanted his mouth against hers and captured her tongue, duelling with it. Eirene felt herself open up like a flower. She held on tightly to him, running her hands over his body and filing away every sensation, every texture in her mind to keep with her during the lonely days ahead.

Eirene thought she saw pain flash across Finn's face, but it disappeared quickly. She looked deep into his eyes and let all the love she had for him shine through. He inhaled sharply.

She smiled through the tears that continued to fall to the sides of her face. This was going to be the last time she'd have him with her. As much as her mind screamed at her for being a fool, she was going to show Finn how much she loved him.

And then she'd let him go.

She cupped his face.

"Oh, Eirene," Finn said against her mouth. "I do love my mate, but she just doesn't get it."

Eirene moved her mouth away from his to look at him confused.

"But you said you loved me."

"Exactly."

"Hold on. You love me and you love your mate."

"More than anything."

"But how can you love both—"

Something in Eirene's mind flashed. She suddenly felt breathless, her throat suddenly thick with emotion. She placed her palms on Finn's chest. Underneath her right palm, Finn's heart beat strong and true. Her belly tightened when he grinned at her. He bent to whisper in her ear.

"You are my mate, Eirene Spence. You are the one I love." Finn's tongue teased her ear, making her shudder. "However, the decision to take me as your mate is yours alone. I can never force you."

A quiver surged through her veins as the impact of Finn's words finally sank in. His face hovered over hers. She searched his countenance only to see the truth of his words, as well as his hunger for her. It made the gold flecks in his eyes stand out like stars.

Eirene caressed Finn's jaw, tracing a path down the column of his neck to the corded muscles of his shoulder underneath his open shirt. She rubbed her palms over his chest, caressing the hard muscles of his pecs before teasing his taut nipples with her thumbs.

"What's your answer, Eirene?"

She smiled when she saw how difficult it was for him not to touch her. A cheeky thought came to mind.

Let him sweat a little. Let him become more aroused. Let him lose control by surrendering to her touch.

"I've made up my mind."

She pushed him gently back on the bed. Heat suffused her cheeks and her channel implored her to let him sink into her. The longing in his eyes only fuelled her own desire. Her robe parted to show the inner curve of her breasts. She straddled Finn's denim encased legs and looked at him.

"How much time do we have before we need to go?"

Finn reached out to open her robe. She stopped him.

"No, Finn Qualtrough."

He growled, but brought his hands down obediently by his hips.

Eirene arched an eyebrow, her eyes filled with mischief.

"How much time?" she repeated.

"About three."

"Three minutes? Three hours?" Her eyes danced

with sensual amusement. "Three seconds?"
"Eirene," Finn warned. "You're playing with fire."

CHAPTER THIRTEEN

His mate was a minx.

"Three hours."

Finn's cock twitched when he heard Eirene's tinkling laughter.

"Enough time," she said, looking at him through her lashes while her hands skimmed his heated skin. The tears were gone, but her warm brown eyes looked like luminous pools of arousal. Finn wanted to drown in them. To sink deep and find her most valuable treasures.

Her heart and her soul.

He hissed when she bent to lick his nipples with her tongue. Ancients! Couldn't she see he was dying to make love to her?

You weren't forthright, Qualtrough. You're getting a dose of your own medicine.

He closed his eyes and groaned. His mate was a tease. There was no way he could stop his mouth from curving into a lopsided grin. He was going to enjoy making her cry out and climax until they were both spent and sated.

He watched Eirene through half lidded eyes. He stifled another groan when she hovered over him to shuck his shirt from his shoulders. He rose up, wanting to get his mouth and tongue on the sweet, creamy flesh of her breasts.

"No, Finn," she said, her breath sweet and soft over him.

He growled louder. His rock hard member strained from the confines of his jeans. His mouth watered when Eirene's honeyed scent of arousal reached his nose. He looked down her parted robe. Her trimmed mound was open as she straddled his legs. Her nether lips were plump and damp. His breath came out in a whoosh as she continued to put her hands all over him. He was clay and she the sculptress, running her hands down his waist. He let out a deep, rumbling groan that almost sounded musical when her fingers trailed over the muscular "V" of his groin. She had hit a tripwire and tiny explosions of lust rippled through him and his stiff cock. His hips almost bucked off the bed when she bent down to place sucking kisses over his belly.

"Eirene." Finn felt her mouth widen to a smile before she stuck her tongue out to encircle his navel. Her glorious tresses partially obstructed his view. Excitement flared inside him when he saw Eirene take his jeans zipper. He drew a harsh breath as he felt her wet tongue lick every little inch of his dick that the zipper exposed.

"Eirene, please let me see."

She hummed in the negative and the sound vibrated through his shaft. He hissed. Shit, he was about to spill! Finn didn't know how long he could last. In a daze he saw Eirene look up at him and arrange her partially dry hair over her shoulder to allow him to watch this time. Finn groaned when Eirene's tongue darted out to lick his shaft and lap at the slit oozing with his pre-cum.

"Mmmmm...you taste good," she said, looking up at him. "I like salty."

After that, she positioned her mouth over his cock head. Her lips lightly brushed against his rod, but not quite on him. She hooked her thumbs over the sides of his jeans.

"Damn! What are you doing, woman?" He rasped.

Instead of answering him, she brought her thumbs down on the waistband of his jeans to push them over his thighs. As he lifted his hips, his dick slid into her mouth, and Eirene hummed in delight. Her cheeks hollowed as she sucked hard, her lips tightening around it with the intensity of her need and demand.

Finn gave a guttural shout, as the power of his orgasm caught him by surprise. He jerked underneath her mouth and gripped Eirene's head, trying to stop her, but she continued to milk him, swallowing every little bit he gave. Her head continued to bob over his gratified rod. Suddenly, his heart skipped a beat as a million sensations descended on him. Everything became bright, like prisms coming from a multifaceted diamond. But the light didn't blind him.

With one last lick which made him shudder, Eirene sat up. Her eyes were dilated with desire, her mouth swollen and parted after indulging him, and her skin was flushed. An aura of opalescent light surrounded her. Finn looked down at his arms. He too was bathed in the same light.

Then he knew.

This was the second part of finding his true mate. The first one was when he stamped Eirene with his scent. The realization hit him square in the chest, overwhelming him for the briefest second.

He was now ready for the third and final step.

Eirene smiled. Her body throbbed with the desire to have Finn fill her. Her nipples puckered and yearned for his hands. Teasing him the way she had was such a turn on. She was Finn's mate.

And he loved her.

At first she hadn't been sure she had heard him correctly when he'd said he loved her. It had taken a few moments for it to sink in and to realize she'd given herself so much heartache for nothing. Everything was so much better than she could have ever dreamed.

She must be the only person in the world to be jealous of her own self.

Finn held her shoulders and gently brought her down to his chest. His hand slid around her nape before he kissed her. Shivers of pleasure travelled down her spine to flood her channel. His kiss burned her, his tongue claimed her. He laid her back and widened the opening of her robe. Her breath came in puffs as he cupped her breast before he tweaked her nipple. She arched her back even while Finn trailed hot wet kisses down her throat. She clung to his broad shoulders, sighing when his tongue found its way to her nipples, flicking and laving them, before taking each one alternately into his mouth. Eirene's hips bucked against his hardness. Her vagina clenched as rapture slammed through her channel.

"Finn, I need you."

Finn stood in front of her. In a daze she watched him undress. His dark gaze raked her naked body, causing her breath to catch in her throat. Her own gaze roamed Finn's muscled physique, from the hard planes of his chest to his strong stomach, down to his pelvis. Counting her blessings, she admired his delicious erection, the instrument of her pleasure. Just looking at him and anticipating the joy he'd give her filled her with excitement and longing.

He was all hers.

Forever.

Finn gripped her hips and brought her to the edge of the bed, making her squeal and giggle. Her heart somersaulted inside her chest. She looked at him and squirmed as he knelt and stared at her sex glistening with liquid heat. Moaning, she closed her eyes when she saw and felt Finn part her lips with his finger.

"You are so beautiful," he growled.

The rough pad of his thumb brushed and encircled her engorged clit before he placed two fingers into her channel, stroking her in and out.

"God! I love the way your fingers feel inside of me."

Eirene's hips writhed against his fingers, glorying at the pleasure spike. She followed the tempo of his thrusts. There was no way she could hold back the small sounds of arousal as he fingered, caressed and pampered her tender opening. She pressed her sex urgently against his fingers, fire blazing through her veins like the hottest lava. Every part of her was consumed by the growing conflagration inside her. Eirene thrashed her head from side to side, moaning, her hands curled into fists on the covers.

"Yield, babe. Yield to me."

Eirene's mind vaguely registered Finn's words before she arched with a cry of rapture as his tongue replaced his thumb.

"Oh, God! Finn!" Eirene cried as Finn continued to piston his fingers in and out of her, his mouth closed over her sensitive flesh. He alternated with gently sucking on her nub to licking it at a fast pace, specifically designed to drive her mad. Her body grew taut, feeling her climax cresting. Finn played her, plucked her, strummed her. A coil of absolute ecstasy gripped her until her whimpers reached a crescendo and she screamed her orgasm. She held on to his head. The feel of his hair in her fingers added to the bliss which overcame her. Her very soul shattered into a million bright pieces before it joined together again to allow her to ride the wave of another orgasm that assaulted her even before the last one subsided.

Finn was rock stiff. The mewls and cries which came forth from Eirene's mouth fueled his lust and his need to join with her.

He encircled an arm around Eirene's waist to bring her to the middle of the bed. Then he crawled over her and kissed her hard. She moaned as she played, sucked, and tasted herself on his tongue. Next, he blazed a trail of open mouthed kisses down her neck, positioning himself in her opening. He clenched his jaw, his balls tightening and his dick aching with the urgency of his need. He hissed when Eirene teased the head with her wet slit.

"Finn, please," she begged, gripping his waist. "I can't stand it. I need you inside of me. I want to bond with you. Please, Finn, mate with me. Make me complete."

Finn growled in response. Eirene didn't need to tell him twice. With one push he thrust inside her and seated himself to the hilt. He groaned at the same time Eirene cried softly against his neck, then her head fell back on the bed. He felt her hands slide down his lower back to grasp his buttocks. She arched her back and urged him on when he took her nipple into his mouth, his tongue swirling over and around the sweet peak as he started to move in and out of her. Her hair was a glorious blue black curtain against the cream sheets.

Soon they danced their own erotic dance. Hips moving out before coming together in unison.

"Look at me, Eirene," he bit out harshly.

Her eyes flew open.

"I want to see you come, and when you do, I need to bite and suck your neck."

She inhaled sharply. It wasn't fear that Finn saw darken her now deep brown eyes. It was her wholehearted trust that he would do the right thing. Finn was humbled.

Finn felt his cock thicken and lengthen. Eirene gasped, then smiled as she felt the change. He continued to thrust in and out of her core. Slowly, languidly, he withdrew and buried himself deep, making them both moan at the pleasure and frisson of skin against skin. Finn's heart pounded at the sheer satisfaction of feeling his cock sink into Eirene's sheath. He loved the snug feel of her sex around him, like an incredibly sweet glove with nerve endings that pleasured each and every bit of his rod. In and out, sliding up and down, he rotated his hips, and every time his balls hit the outside of her vagina Eirene moaned. The scent of her sex drove him wild. The scent of their joint musk filled the air. The sweat of their bodies a light film of still unfulfilled desire.

"More, Finn. I want more, babe. Take me harder."

Finn groaned as a surge of lust forged through his cock. He moved, hitting her inside harder. Deeper. Then faster. Eirene urged him on, begging for more. She closed her eyes.

"Eirene!"

"I have to. It feels so damn good!"

Eirene arched her back and whimpered as he pounded into her. The intensity of the sensations that suffused him tightened his balls. He plunged into her sweet addictive heat. Over and over again they came together, the aura of their mating swirling around them until Eirene screamed. The sound sharpened Finn's canines. He lowered his mouth to the pulse on her neck. He swirled his tongue around the skin before he sucked and bit. As soon as he tasted just a drop of her blood, he felt his head almost explode, his manhood releasing its load into Eirene. That tiny drop was enough, but he continued to suck and lick on her pulse, his body jerking with the force of his release. Eirene completely belonged to him now. He completely belonged to her.

It was the most incredible experience in his damned

immortal existence.

But he wasn't damned now, Finn thought as he continued to move inside Eirene until he lay on her, waiting for his heartbeat to return to its normal pace. He smiled against her neck. She too was breathing hard, slowly bringing her heart rate down. Eirene would be with him. The wall around his heart finally cracked and fell in a heap. With their mating he had infused her with his immortality. By tasting even just a drop of her blood he had built a connection to her. He would know where she was as she would always be aware of him. He could rebuild his life now. His heart constricted at the thought she might disappear just like his parents had disappeared, but that wouldn't happen now that they were connected in every way. His heart swelled with relief, and as he lifted his head to look at his mate's ecstatic and blissful face, his entire being flooded with love for her.

* * * *

Finn was still inside of her. Her channel still twitched and clenched. Her clit still throbbed from the heat of their passion and she felt liquid desire flow again through her channel.

She did not know what it meant when Finn bit her. Part of her tensed at the thought of fangs digging into her neck, but she had been in such throes of ecstasy that when Finn's teeth had sunk into her at the same time his cock had surged into her vagina, the orgasm she experienced had been mind-altering. All she could do was ride the fulfilment that consumed her. She didn't know where she ended and where Finn began. When she'd felt Finn pulling blood from her neck while at the same time spurting his seed into her, she had felt her soul lock with his. As his essence flowed into her, she'd seen his life flash before her eyes and witness the last time Finn had seen his parents. She squeezed her eyes tighter, her heart breaking for him.

Tears poured from beneath her eyelids, falling down the sides of her face. When he stiffened, they both knew his memories now belonged to her too.

"I'm so sorry," she whispered in his ear, running her fingers through his short hair before holding him closer to her.

"It was a long time ago, Eirene."

"Still. No child should lose their parents. In any way."

Finn lifted his head and looked down on her.

"And no man should kiss and tell and treat you the way that bastard did," he said, giving her a tight smile. She now knew her memories were his also.

Eirene ran her hand up and down his bicep.

"We're such a pair, aren't we?"

Finn chuckled. Eirene moaned and her hips bucked when Finn's low laughter vibrated down to her sex.

She wanted him again.

Her inner muscles clenched around Finn's incredible manhood, causing him to groan. She sighed when he pushed his shaft in again before he finally withdrew.

"Why?" she asked in disappointment.

Finn chuckled, then turned her onto her belly and lifted her hips.

"Hhhmmm," she hummed, wiggling her hips. She noticed he was still semi-hard, his rod wet with their joint cream. She sighed with a smile as Finn sheathed himself into her sex once more. A low growl rumbled from his chest when her sex clasped tightly around him.

Then he unsheathed himself until only the head

remained at Eirene's entrance before he thrust hard and deep into her. A bolt of rapture shot into his hard rod. He did it again, incited by Eirene's moans, and grunted in satisfaction when she whimpered. Quick and short, deep and long, Finn changed the way he made love to her so that Eirene was at a loss at what to expect. Faster and faster he went, and when Eirene was about to come he stopped, withdrawing from her.

"Oh, God, Finn. Please!" Then she gave another cry when Finn's fingers found her clit and played with it. Fast. Then he thrust into her again.

He bent down to whisper in her ear.

"Yield."

"I am," she moaned.

"Yield," he said once more as he continued to plunge into her channel. He felt her lessen her hold on him and open up.

Completely.

Finn closed his eyes. The pulse on the base of his neck and the beat of his heart fused with Eirene's. She mewled and her cries increased. He gripped her waist, his thrusts becoming shorter and faster. He gasped and growled when his member was balls deep.

Eirene held on for dear life, gripping the sheets tightly in her hands as wave upon wave of bliss washed over her. Her breasts felt heavy as they jiggled underneath her with Finn's every thrust. Her body was sensitized with the intense pleasure of Finn's shaft inside her, branding her so that her body would never seek anyone else. He claimed her. She was his in every way. His fingers on her clit added to the inexplicable rapture that thrummed through her. Finn thrust faster and faster. Eirene cried out, her orgasm was upon her even before she knew it, and she sobbed Finn's name over and over again. With one more thrust, Finn shouted her name as he emptied himself into her. His strength mixed with her warmth. It was moments later their orgasms let go of their grip and they fell on the bed together, slowly drifting to an exhausted sleep.

CHAPTER FOURTEEN

As soon as they entered the nerve centre a chorus of elated and happy greetings met them, bringing a blush to Eirene's cheeks. Finn had to curb the wave of jealousy that rolled over him at seeing his brothers welcome his mate with warm hugs. They wouldn't do anything to her, except protect her.

One wrong move and they were dead.

"Finn." Roarke strode to him. His eyes were filled with amusement. "It can't be that bad."

"Oh, it is bad," he muttered. "I just want her all to myself."

Roarke laughed quietly.

"But she is yours. Nothing can break your bond now."

Finn looked at his leader and saw the sadness flash in Roarke's silver blue eyes before it vanished.

"Let's get started, shall we?" Roarke nudged him, his mouth quirked to a half smile while he rubbed the centre of his chest.

Finn watched as Roarke moved towards the huge table of African Blackwood filled with several maps and rolled parchments. It stood as an incongruous divider between the computer area and the overstuffed arm chairs and couch which flanked the huge fireplace. Now that Finn knew the happiness of finding Eirene, he wished that same happiness for the man he called brother. The death of Roarke's mate had been more than two hundred years before the Hamiltons had taken him in after his uncle, a friar and a Cynn mortal, had died. Roarke never spoke about her, but Finn hoped that someday he could move on.

His mouth curved into a light grin. Who would have thought he'd become a softie after Eirene? She had changed him. She had brought back the light in his life when he thought he'd never find it again. She was also his kick-ass woman and he couldn't have anyone better by his side than her.

Finn couldn't remove his eyes from his mate as he stood by the bannister of the spiral staircase. He'd had her only a mere half hour ago and his dick was already begging to be inside her again.

"Be still, my beating cock," he muttered underneath his breath.

He heard Eirene chuckle softly from across the room.

I heard that.

Finn grinned at his mate, whose sexy back was turned to him. And damn did she look sexy. Black really suited her. Her tank top was a perfect foil for her creamy skin. It showed off her toned arms and beautiful shoulders. It hugged her body like a second skin, showing off the perfect shape of her breasts, the curve of her waist, skimming her flat belly. Finn felt another wave of irrational jealousy at the clingy material. It could caress her body in front of everybody. If he did that, he would have been hauled off for public indecency. Her hips and thighs were encased in black stretch jeans tucked into medium heeled black leather L.K. Bennett boots. Her breasts, which he longed to cup again, were gently squeezed into her bra underneath a tank that pushed them up and allowed the top of the perfect globes to gently swell over her neckline. Finn wanted to dip his tongue into her cleavage while he rubbed and pinched her nipples into button hardness. Hell, he wanted to bed her right then and there.

Stop it!

Finn arched his brow.

Why? If I can't have you now, I can always

fantasize, can't I?

Because I'm really wet here and I can't concentrate.

Finn smiled. *Glad I'm not the only one suffering.*

Eirene giggled so suddenly that Graeme gave her a bemused look.

You're insatiable.

So are you, Eirene. So are you.

"Okay, if you two lovebirds are done with your telepathic sex, I suggest we decide what our best course of action is," Roarke stated with a wry grin.

Blake chuckled, then kept it to a minimum when Finn glared at him.

"C'mon, Finn. Lighten up."

Finn exhaled the tension in his shoulders.

"Someday, Strachan, I will be the one laughing when you meet your mate."

Blake guffawed. "Not going to happen in the next two hundred. I'm still enjoying the life of a single stud."

"Just make sure you don't acquire anything contagious," Zac spoke. Blake reddened.

"Thanks, Zac," Blake mumbled.

"Eirene. You have the floor."

Finn noticed the blush on Eirene's cheeks and the dusky rosiness of her mouth. She probably wasn't used to this kind of ribbing. He was going to enjoy teaching her all the ways of the Cynn.

"I've set up your computer system, but didn't know how to access Dac's signal," Graeme informed her.

Eirene smiled, her eyes twinkling.

"I wouldn't be good at what I do if even one person found it easy to break through my set up."

Blake coughed, covering his mouth with his hand.

"Sorry," he wheezed. "Something stuck. Inside…throat."

Eirene bit the inside of her cheek to stifle her grin.

"As you all know I created a program for Dac, not realizing he was a Scatha Cruor." Eirene began.

"Did Dac approach you for the program?"

"Not exactly," she hesitated. "I broke into his system."

Blake whistled. Eirene looked at Finn. There was admiration in her mate's eyes.

"I actually couldn't make heads or tails of Dac's system," she admitted. "Numbers that created symbols within the program was messing with my head."

"That can't happen." Graeme shook his head emphatically.

"That's what I thought." Eirene agreed. "But look..."

Eirene's fingers flew over the keyboard and the symbols she'd previously uncovered appeared on the computer screen.

Graeme whistled softly, eyes alight with interest as he looked at the symbols.

"That's a first. How did you know they were symbols?"

"My father, my adoptive father that is, was a scholar of semiotics. If there was anything he shared with me it was his interest in the field."

Eirene thought of her adoptive sire. She never received any affection from him or his wife, but when they discussed his scholarly interest, a fragile bond was created between them. Sometimes it was the only thing keeping her sane while she lived with them. And for developing her interest in semiotics, she was grateful.

I'm so sorry, babe.

Eirene pressed her lips together in a semblance of a smile as she looked at her mate.

It's okay, Finn. It was a long time ago.

Finn nodded, respecting her need to keep the

memories to herself.

Eirene looked at the faces of the rest of the Cynn. All their faces were grim.

"Why did you do that?" Graeme frowned.

Eirene turned her chair back to face the computer. Her fingers flew over the keyboard once more. Immediately several boxes came up of different locations in Manchester and around the U.K. on the huge LED screen on the wall. She pointed to the screen.

"All these are the programs I made for clients. Most of these clients are big corporations with a less than stellar reputations. Devon and I have been looking for a particular system that will help him."

"Help him what?" Blake asked.

Eirene turned back to them.

"Find his daughter. She was ten years old when she and Janice, her mother, disappeared."

"When was this?" Zac asked, his brow furrowed in concern.

"Almost five years ago."

The silence was deafening before softly said swear words filled the air.

"Why did you decide to look at organizational computer systems?" Roarke asked.

"Because they suddenly disappeared without a trace." Eirene swivelled her chair to face the keyboard again. In seconds, a grainy CCTV footage of a woman with a young girl filled the screen. "This is footage I was able to get from the Manchester Airport's system, of Janice and Penny on their way to catch their plane. They never took any flight leaving that day."

"Why would they go to the airport and then not take any flight at all?" Finn moved towards Eirene.

"I can't say why but I can't help but feel that they were trying to lose their tail."

"Tail?" Blake prompted. "Someone was following them?"

"Not sure about that either. What I do know is that the next footage you will see is of Janice and Penny leaving the Manchester airport fifteen minutes after they arrived."

Eirene looked away. If she didn't, the anger she felt the first time she saw the video would surface again and she might just smash something.

Suddenly, she felt Finn's warm hands massage her shoulders.

"I'm sorry," she spoke for the benefit of the others. "I cannot watch this footage again. It just makes me so angry seeing Janice manhandle Penny that way. Devon hasn't seen this yet. I don't want him to relapse and feel he has nothing to live for."

"Understood." Roarke replied.

Eirene looked up at Finn standing beside her. He grazed her lower lip with his thumb, and she kissed the pad and smiled. She pressed "Enter", refusing to look at the screen.

Another grainy clip appeared on the screen. This time Penny was being dragged by her mother into a waiting Volvo XC90 SUV.

"Holy shit."

Eirene looked at Blake. All of the Cynn Cruors including Finn stared at the footage. All their faces hard. Furious.

"Finn, you're hurting me."

Finn's grip on her shoulder loosened. The anger in his eyes disappeared replaced with self-reproach. He bent down and kissed the spot he had gripped on her shoulder.

"I'm sorry, Eirene. I didn't mean to."

"I know you didn't, babe," she said, standing up to

cup his face. She saw the rest of the warriors walk around like caged lions. Only Finn and Roarke stood where they were.

"Are the weapons ready?" Roarke's voice was devoid of emotion, his face a harsh mask of anger as he continued to look at the footage that replayed itself on the wall.

Finn nodded. "Polished and ready. Have been for quite some time."

"Eirene, can you zero in on Dac's coordinates again, please?"

"What have the Cynn mortals reported?" Blake asked, his face flinty, his boyish and joking demeanour gone.

Graeme faced Blake as he stood. He shook his head.

"No activity at all," he replied. "It's a warehouse in Trafford Park, but they haven't noticed anything unusual."

Eirene pivoted to the keyboard. Fingers flying again over the keys, the rest of the programs disappeared, leaving only one red point blinking.

"He hasn't left," she said.

Roarke gave a curt nod. "Let's plan."

"C'mon, babe." Finn took her hand and brought her with him towards the table. Eirene felt the cold anger inside him.

"I think all of you know what you have to do." Roarke began. Eirene listened to what they planned to do, but they were talking too softly and too fast for her to keep up. Finally, the discussion ended. Graeme, Blake, Zac, and Finn moved through one of the long row of bookshelves and came back with different kinds of assault weapons. She sucked in her breath at the sight of Finn' long sword which he sheathed behind his back and the sniper rifle he held tucked under his arm. All the others also had their own swords which looked like heirloom pieces. Everyone wore shirts underneath their jackets. Save for their weapons, they looked like they were dressed for a night on the town.

Except for their assault weapons.

"We will help you find Devon's daughter tonight," Roarke said, looking at her. His eyes were hard as flint. "Finn, I'll meet you downstairs."

Finn nodded before he turned back to Eirene.

"Shouldn't I go with you?" Eirene asked, the muscle inside her chest constricting at the thought of Finn in danger. "Isn't a Cynn Cruor's mate supposed to stand by him when there's a fight?"

Finn shook his head. He quirked his mouth in a rueful smile. "I would love for you to join me, but no one will be left here with Devon. We need someone here in the centre to track our whereabouts."

Eirene sighed reluctantly before she nodded.

"Alright," she said. "But how can you find Penny tonight when you're after Dac?"

"Because the people who took Penny were Scatha Cruors, Eirene. Dac has Penny."

CHAPTER FIFTEEN

Dac was furious as he paced the entire length of his opulent office. At the moment the walnut panelled walls of the room reminded him of the grills of a cell underneath the coliseum. He had imprisoned many Christians in those cells before feeding them to deliberately starved and voraciously hungry beasts for the entertainment of the Romans.

In all his immortal life no one had bested him. The Cynn Cruors had been hard pressed to find him, and every time he had escaped detection. He had the best evil geniuses in his pockets and they took the fall for him. He was invincible, had everything at his disposal. No one could defeat him. Not even the Cynn Eald.

Until now.

Dac never expected to be trumped by someone with a razor sharp computer mind. It was why he wanted to meet the programmer. He had underestimated the solicitor. Devon had been the first solicitor he'd met in a very long time who stuck to a very strong code of ethics. He had a moral compass and Dac had to grudgingly respect him for that. He'd been about to find out Devon's weakness when the Cynn Cruors had arrived. He had successfully evaded them for centuries. How did they find out he was in Manchester?

Unless there was a mole in his organization.

Dac's eyes changed colour as his fury took over. His blood boiled with an all-consuming hatred which had allowed him to survive for centuries. Herod, his right hand, would find the transfuge and when he did, Dac would personally torture him to death in front of all the Scatha and their mortal slaves. Insubordination had no place in his empire. They would have the freedom they craved.

But it was his divine right to bestow that freedom.

He stopped prowling. The thud, thud of loud music below vibrated against the wooden, but carpeted floor. Freddie, a computer whiz faced the laptop they had brought with them to Devon's office a few days ago. His eyes darted furtively over the monitor as beads of sweat formed on his forehead.

"I thought you said the program worked," Dac bit out.

"It did. It was working." Freddie pressed down hard on the "Enter" button, but nothing happened. "I don't understand it. It worked perfectly when we got it."

Dac roared. Freddie winced. He kept his eyes on the screen so Dac couldn't see his fear.

Dac smiled. "You think I don't smell your fear, you pathetic excuse for a Scatha?"

Freddie paled.

"Don't worry; I still have use of you. You won't die today."

The computer expert visibly swallowed as he continued his attempts at retrieving the program.

Herod sat unruffled by the edge of the huge oak table.

"A safety must have been included in the program," he commented with detachment, keeping his eye on his liege lord.

Dac glared at him with annoyance. Among his followers, only Herod had balls big enough to be able to stand up to him. He had been instrumental in helping Dac escape after the foiled assassination attempt on the Ancient Cynn. It was Herod who told Dac about the Deoré but he made a mistake of believing that he was invincible and had paid the price.

"Keep talking," he commanded as his eyes narrowed into blood red slits.

Herod shrugged.

"No payment, no program. Looks like the person has destroyed the program or has suspended the activation of the last part of the program."

Dac swore in all the new and ancient languages known to man in rapid fire succession before punching a hole in the wall. This unknown programmer was going to cost him millions and he hated parting with his money. This couldn't happen. Without that program, his organization's system would be vulnerable to any attack, particularly from his enemies and the authorities. They would find out where the missing children were, whom Dac had sold to prostitution, and they would find out the number of people he had killed. He couldn't afford that, not because he was afraid of getting caught by mortals. He couldn't afford to allow his face, no matter how blurred, to grace the evening news. If the Cynn Cruors just saw a glimpse of any footage with him in it, they would all converge and kill him. His movements would become limited again, just like the days after he had barely escaped with his life.

"Find that damn solicitor," he shouted. "Do whatever you have to get the name of the programmer, then kill that bastard. Kill them both."

CHAPTER SIXTEEN

There was radio silence, everyone intent on the mission. Finn surveyed the back door of Dac's club called *Dare You!* atop the opposite building. It was located in an industrial estate in Trafford Park that was two miles southwest of Manchester city. Surrounded by factories which looked like eerie behemoths rising against the dark starless sky, the place should have closed down a long time ago. But the pull of being away from the bustle of the city to go to a secret place was enough for the more adventurous to converge and be seen in Dac's club.

Finn looked down. Two of the Scatha Cruor came out to smoke weed, their voices loud with ribald humour. Their hips moved back and forth as each one told their stories of how many women they were able to hook up with inside the club. The climaxes of the women had melded with the shouts and laughter of the oblivious patrons.

Finn continued his survey of the area. The top floor of the club's building was lit up, but Finn couldn't see what was happening inside because the blinds were drawn.

"Alpha, Dac might probably be on the top floor," he said, calling Roarke by his field name. "The blinds are closed, but I sense a lot of activity. A lot of agitation and anger."

"Temple and Strachan, you know what to do," Roarke said.

Finn trained his sniper's scope at the windows of the top most floor hoping to find a gap where he could at least see a little of what was happening inside. Then his heart gave such a hard thump that he unconsciously took a small step back. A frisson trickled down his spine and his senses suddenly became more alert. Finn frowned. Eirene? His razor sharp eyes narrowed to survey the area. His mate couldn't be here. Just as he was about to make another sweep of the area, the feeling disappeared. Finn shook his head slightly to clear his mind and retrained his sniper's scope on the window.

"We're by the fire escape on the top floor," Blake said, all humour gone from his voice. "Approaching the door."

"McBain, with me," Roarke said.

From his vantage point, Finn saw Roarke pass Zac, who immediately fell into step with his leader. They split up in the middle of the street, Zac walking towards the entrance while Roarke continued to the back of the building. Both kept their eyes trained on the Scatha bouncers. Using their gift of cloaking themselves, the bouncers hardly noticed them as they continued to ogle the female patrons' low tops which allowed them enticing views of their breasts.

Seconds ticked like minutes.

Finn honed his sniper's scope back on the activity on the top floor as he cradled the AX338 sniper rifle in his hands. His ears pricked when he heard Dac shout out orders to find Eirene. Cold dread laced around his heart. The Scatha still didn't know it was Eirene who had made the program. They would soon.

And then they would get their filthy hands on his sweet Eirene.

His mate.

Not in this lifetime. Not if he had to kill every one of them with his bare hands.

"Dux, Dac has just ordered a hit on both Eirene and Devon," Finn said, trying to remove the panic in his voice, but couldn't.

"Easy, Qualtrough," Roarke said. "We'll get Dac,

and once we do, we'll send him back to the Council of Ieldran to stand trial."

"Hold it right there."

They all heard Graeme before the fight broke out. Finn swore before he jumped the distance to smash against the windows of the top floor. He grunted in pain as he slammed through the glass and rolled on the floor to break the impact. Finn heard a roar from his left so he rolled to the right and sat on his hunches with his rifle trained to where the sound came from. It was Dac's companion, Freddie. His face contorted as his mouth widened to become a jowl full of razor sharp teeth, while his hands transformed into claws. He roared his anger. Finn turned his face away.

"Use any mouthwash lately?" He taunted. "I doubt there's anything strong enough to remove your stench."

Freddie keened in fury before landing on Finn. The sniper rifle was thrown away from him. Finn threw Freddie back with a huge shove. Even before he had launched himself back on his feet, he had unsheathed his silver bladed sword, swinging it over his head. He turned and grinned when he saw Freddie hesitate. That was more than enough time. Finn jumped, twisted in mid-air and sliced downward to decapitate Freddie. He raised his arm to cover his eyes as Freddie's ashes swirled around. Finn stood up and shook the glass from his body. The slashes made by the glass on his exposed skin ejected the debris from the wound and closed.

"Stupid bastard," he muttered.

Then he heard a deep throaty laugh.

"I never thought I'd see the day to find myself face to face with the Qualtrough spawn."

Rage like no other spread through Finn as he whipped around. His eyes glazed over, his pupils dilated with the colour of bloodlust. He held his sword tightly, the knuckles of his right hand white with strain.

"Is that the best that you can do?" Finn mocked, trying to guard his heart from the pain of his parents' memory. "Today you either stand trial or die, Dac. It doesn't matter to me. And tomorrow, the Scatha will be no more."

Dac's completely eyes burned with hatred.

"If I die, then you will never know where the rest of the Scatha are."

Finn barked with laughter which didn't reach his eyes.

"If you die, the Scatha will scatter. Without a leader everything you built can be destroyed. The Cynn Cruors will see to that."

"No one will take away what belongs to me," Dac hissed with fury. "The Cynn Cruors have always been weak. Your opting to blend with the mortals when we are all much better than them was your fatal mistake."

Dac sniffed, his eyes gleaming with knowledge. Finn gritted his teeth and closed his mind against Dac's onslaught.

"You have found a mate."

"I have not."

Dac laughed, an eerie and piercing chortle that hurt Finn's ears. Quickly Finn rolled towards the sniper rifle as he sheathed his sword. He lifted his weapon and fired. Dac gave a blood curdling scream as he was thrown off balance. Finn approached him slowly. He held the sniper rifle in his left hand and again unsheathed his sword with his right hand. Blood oozed from a wound in the centre of Dac's chest.

Suddenly Finn heard running steps coming towards him. He whirled around. It was Roarke and Zac with their swords drawn. Behind them, he saw Graeme let go of his gun to tend to Blake's wounds. Blake was ashen as he stared into space.

"Finn, look out!" Roarke flew fast towards Finn, but he was too late. Finn let out a shout of agony as he felt metal like claws enter one side and rip him through the other side of his lower body. Dazed, he looked down. He felt his blood cascade from the deep gashes on his lower back like a weak fountain. He fell on his knees before falling forward.

"Zac!" Roarke shouted.

In the midst of it all they saw Dac stand. Blood oozed from the side of his mouth, but he was cackling with glee.

"Fucking fools! I thrive on pain," he screamed as he continued to laugh before he jumped out of the window. Everyone shielded their faces as more glass splattered into the room.

Finn tried to fight the blackness threatening him. He had never felt such agony as he did now. He thought of Eirene. He had to keep her safe. He had to tell Roarke.

"Eirene," he shouted at Roarke, but his voice only came out as a whisper.

"She's safe, Finn," Roarke said grimly. "We need to get you back to the Faesten. Preserve your strength."

"She's not safe," Finn bit out. "Dac. He knows who she is. Need to protect her."

Then darkness finally won.

CHAPTER SEVENTEEN

Devon came down from his room minutes after the warriors left to capture Dac. Eirene immediately killed the CCTV footage of Penny, but not quickly enough. She had no choice but to tell Devon the truth.

"I'm sorry, Devon. I didn't want you to get hurt."

"Eirene, I'm a father who has been looking for his daughter for a long time, not a diva."

Eirene couldn't suppress her giggle.

"You're stronger than I thought," she said.

Devon shrugged, wincing a little. "I have to be."

Eirene told Devon about Dac and his possible connection to Penny's kidnapping.

"I have to follow them." Eirene stood up. She had earlier concealed her baton and butterfly knife in the inner pocket of her hoodie, thinking she would be joining the Cynn warriors to fight Dac.

"Why?"

"If Dac is busy with the warriors, I might be able to find something more about Penny's whereabouts."

"I'm not quite sure," Devon said, frowning as he mulled over what Eirene was planning to do.

"Devon, this is also our chance to find Penny. You've been waiting for so long."

Devon looked at Eirene before he came to a decision.

"Okay," he conceded. "What do you want me to do?"

"Stay here in the nerve centre and keep an eye on everybody. I have my mobile phone. I will keep you posted. You've been to the office in my house so the controls here are the same."

Devon nodded.

Eirene strode to the glass doors.

"Eirene?"

"Yes?" she asked, turning back to Devon.

"I hope you find my Penny."

Eirene gave him a tight smile. Her heart bled at Devon's lost look.

"I will do my best."

* * * *

Eirene remained in the shadows until the Cynn left their posts.

"Finn is going to kill me," she muttered to herself. With their newly found connection Eirene had to make sure to shield her mind. She winced. If Finn knew she had followed them, there was no telling what he would do. She was certain he wouldn't hurt her. Her mouth quirked ever so slightly in amusement. He would just have to get used to her tenacity and her stubbornness.

To stop Finn from knowing she was close by, Eirene imagined a wall, a huge stonewall like those seen in the ruined castles of Scotland, surrounding her mind before concentrating on what she had to do. If Dac had Penny, she needed to find out exactly where he was keeping her. Dac would be busy fighting off the Cynn and she'd have time to discover Penny's whereabouts.

Eirene saw Roarke and Graeme stride towards the club and split up in the middle of the road. She wondered where Finn was. She could feel him near, but for Finn not to know she was also in the area, she couldn't allow her mind to reach out too much. She waited for a minute more before leaving the shadows. She tied her hoodie around her waist to make it smaller. Sucking in her breath to make her breasts look slightly bigger, she walked towards the entrance. She almost gagged at the overwhelming stench of the two Scatha bouncers ogling the women who entered the narrow entrance. She shuddered as she saw the women fall under the thrall of the creatures. How the hell could she pull this off? She had no clue, but the thought of Penny being Dac's prisoner for the last seven years spurred her on.

She approached the entrance slowly. Her heeled boots made her hips sway seductively. One of the Scatha saw her approach and faced her as though throwing his charm at her. Eirene squashed the urge to cover her nose. The Scatha may look ruggedly handsome with his bulging biceps and muscled body, but his lascivious smile and sewer smell almost made her dry heave in front of him. Now that she was bound to Finn, all her senses were more acute. Hell, with her strong sense of smell she could probably be a good nose for a perfume company. A long queue snaked its way outside the walls of the Club. Women in tiny sequined dresses and platform heels preened and sashayed to the loud beat of the music filtering out of the Club's doors.

"Hey there, pretty lady," the smelly Scatha greeted her with a grin. "You smell of sex. If you want me, you'll have to fall in line."

Eirene arched a brow. A shudder of revulsion crawled at her insides, but she didn't have much time. Swallowing hard, she stood in front of him, hand on hip. Suddenly, she cupped the front of his pants and let her middle finger trail along his semi-hard rod. Surprise, then lust, flared in the Scatha's eyes, his grin almost feral. She leaned towards him slowly, her stomach almost heaving.

"If you allow me inside right away, I can do more than trace you with my finger," she said softly before moving several feet away to suck fresh air into her lungs.

She heard his low growl. His eyes narrowed at her. When she looked down, she saw his dick was tenting his pants. There were hoots and squeals from some in the long queue who had witnessed Eirene cupping the Scatha. The Scatha's companion grinned as well, his mouth much too wide for his face.

Eirene waited. Her heart fluttered in fear. Did he fall for it? She was just hoping that what Finn had said was true. The Scatha's senses had been dumbed down by the evil they committed. The Scatha moved towards her and grabbed her arm.

"You better make good on your promise, bitch," he growled. "My balls are aching and my cock wants to get better acquainted – much better acquainted with those rosy red lips of yours..."

Eirene closed her eyes, hoping her captor didn't feel her shudder.

Put your filthy member in my mouth and I'll bite so hard on it, you'd wish you were a woman.

Suddenly she heard glass crashing above them. She looked up before raising her arm to shield her face. As the debris started falling, the women in the queue screamed, scattering to get away from the falling shards. The men ran to their cars which immediately roared to life, backing them out away from the club. The Scatha bouncers growled and looked at each other. The creature that held her squeezed her arm.

"You're coming with me."

"Where?"

"Up there!"

"Not on your bloody life!"

With all the force she could muster, she brought her heeled boot down hard on the side of his knee and heard the satisfying crack of bone breaking. The Scatha screamed and let go of her. Eirene ran into the club.

177

Many of the patrons hadn't noticed the ruckus outside as the music had drowned out the noise. She quickly scanned the area over the gyrating bodies on the floor. She saw one heavy man push a curtain away. He was with several men and from Eirene's vantage point, they appeared eager to follow the heavy set man. Eirene made a beeline for the door not bothering to apologize as she pushed her way through the throng. If her spidey hunch was right, Penny might just be inside that door.

"Bloody hell!" she swore when she found the door was locked. She took out her butterfly knife from her back pocket. With a flick of her wrist, it opened and she used it to slowly pry the doorknob from its housing. Before she could finish, the door was opened by the heavy set man. He glared at her.

"What are you—damn bitch!" he bellowed, then was surprised to see the knife imbedded in his chest. There was a scream behind Eirene as one of the women saw what happened. Pandemonium now broke out inside the club as everyone rushed to the club's entrance. Eirene smashed her palm against the Scatha's nose before removing her knife from his chest.

Then she screamed and fell.

Finn!

Bile rose in her throat as she felt the fiery pain in her lower back. She knew Finn was injured.

Eirene.

Finn! I'm here!

Dac...be careful. Find you.

No babe. He won't. Eirene swallowed hard to stop the sobs. Tears started flowing from her eyes. She had to think. God damn it, she wasn't going to let Finn die.

She tried to stand up twice, but got nudged back on the floor. Angrily she pushed against the legs and grabbed at others to stand up. The Scatha she stabbed was gone. Eirene scanned the sides of the club. A group of men who looked like Scatha followed a tall man who came down from a flight of stairs towards an exit. She ran towards the stairs.

The lights were dim. She looked back at the club. No one followed her. Looking up the stairs, she sprinted up. The closer she got to the top, the stronger she felt Finn.

Finn, I'm coming, babe.

Finn didn't reply.

"Damn it, Finn! Don't bloody die on me!" she screamed.

"Eirene?" Roarke looked down from the top floor with incredulity, anger, then relief. He swore. "What the hell are you doing here?"

"Where's Finn?"

A whoosh of air blew her hair away from her sweaty face before Roarke stood beside her.

"You keep on saving your mate time and time again."

"As it should be. Take me to him," Eirene ordered Roarke. She held on to him as Roarke sped to the top floor with her.

Eirene's knees buckled at the sight of Finn surrounded by blood, his face pale.

"Eirene..." Zac began, his face troubled.

"I know, Zac," Eirene said. She forced herself to walk on wooden legs and knelt beside Zac. "Need another knife. I used my blade on a Scatha."

Zac handed her his thin blade. Without hesitation, she slashed her wrist, wincing at the pain. She brought her wrist over Finn's mouth. He didn't move. Eirene brought her wrist closer.

"Finn, baby. Drink. Please drink, my love." Eirene's voice broke, the tears splashing against Finn's chest. She leaned lower and whispered into his ear. "Don't leave me. Please don't leave me, Finn. I love you. C'mon drink."

Zac knelt on the opposite side. He placed his fingers on Finn's throat massaging it so that the blood could enter his system. Roarke, Graeme, and Blake surrounded them, watching grimly.

"Fine! If you don't want to drink, you don't have to leave me. I'm going ahead of you. I will kill myself and you'll never see me again. And I had to wound myself for you, and...oh, God!"

An intense bolt of lust surged through her when Finn's hand grabbed her arm with lightning speed. His razor sharp incisors stung before she felt him draw blood from the vein that felt utterly glorious, bringing bolts of pure pleasure to her clit. She closed her eyes as she bit down on her lower lip, drawing blood to stop the ecstatic moan rolling up her throat. Liquid heat flooded between her thighs. She was close to the precipice. She had never felt this kind of bliss from blood being drawn from her. It was sensual. It was erotic. It was bliss. She closed her eyes as tears fell. She finally understood the bond between Finn and her. The bond between mates, and it transcended everything physical. Her soul was there for Finn to cherish in the same way that Finn would cherish hers. Now their hearts would beat as one for all eternity.

She opened her eyes. Finn's eyes were still closed. His hands had let go of her arm.

"Finn, will be okay." Zac assured her as he bandaged her wrist. "We have to get him out."

She nodded. She winced when she saw Finn's deep wounds but the bleeding had stopped and the flesh, although red, was starting to close albeit at a snail's pace. She untied her hoodie and wrapped it around

Finn's lower back. Satisfied that she had secured her hoodie around Finn's wounds, she stepped aside to allow Roarke to lift his brother in his arms while Zac took Finn's rifle, and she held on to his sword.

CHAPTER EIGHTEEN

The light of the full moon streamed through the windows of the dark room. Finn opened his eyes, slightly disoriented until he realized he was back in the Faesten.

Eirene! He needed to get to her.

Finn threw the covers away from his naked body and got up. He grimaced as his new skin stretched in protest. The memory of blinding pain and Dac washed over him. He had been distracted by Roarke and Zac arriving, thinking they were Scatha. He was such a bloody fool, but the knowledge that Dac knew about Eirene almost paralyzed him with fear.

Finn switched on the bedside lamp before he made his way to the bathroom to shower. He sighed as the water cascaded over his tired muscles, washing the fatigue down the drain. He was in the middle of putting on a shirt when his bedroom door opened, bringing with it a flood of light from the corridor.

"You're awake," Zac noted pleased. "That's good."

"Where's Eirene?"

"Sleeping," Zac replied. "Roarke threatened to bar her from you if she didn't get any rest," he chuckled. "Your mate is one stubborn woman."

The side of Finn's mouth quirked.

"Yes, one stubborn and lovable woman."

"Let me have a look at your wounds."

Finn kept his arms abreast with his chest as Zac checked his wounds.

"They're healing nicely. Good."

Finn brought his T-shirt down, tucking it into his Levi's.

"Roarke wants to speak with you."

Finn hesitated.

"Eirene needs to rest Finn," Zac said firmly. "She's been here the last two days, refusing to leave your side after giving you her blood in Dac's club."

Finn stood stunned. Two days. He was out for two days. His heart plummeted.

"She was in Dac's club? What the bloody hell was she doing there?" Finn asked through gritted teeth. He should have listened to his instincts and realized his mate was a bloody stubborn woman when she put her mind on something. A wave of delayed panic washed over him. If Dac had seen Eirene then he'd be able to put two and two together. The fear that possibility gave him made his blood run cold. His hands balled into fists by his sides.

"It's not for me to tell you."

"Did she—?"

"Yes, a lot. She's a bit weak now. That's why she needs to sleep to recover," Zac answered, but he smiled. "She's a strong woman, Finn. I wish the rest of us were half as lucky to find a mate like her."

"I need to see Eirene first before I speak to Roarke. Please."

After several moments, Zac reluctantly nodded. "I'll tell Roarke." Then his mouth curved in amusement. "Just make sure you don't tire her, mate."

Finn chuckled as he nodded, feeling his face flush. Being embarrassed in front of a fellow Cynn warrior was unheard off. Eirene had really changed him.

After Zac left, Finn finished dressing in a daze. He placed his hands on his hips as he gazed out of the window. People were walking along the pavement, making their way to the clubs that blared their own brand of music.

Oblivious to the continuing war between the Cruors around them.

Eirene had been there for him all the time, even during his most vulnerable moments. She hadn't left. He thought of his parents. Two of the people he had loved the most had left him to keep him safe. He had carried the burden of being left behind for a very long time. The overriding need to kill Dac which fuelled his existence was still there but it was now tempered, thanks to Eirene being by his side. Going after Dac with guns blazing and without a coherent plan was suicide.

He knew that now.

Tempered by his mate's love for him, Eirene had lifted that burden by returning to him over and over again. His parents would have loved her. They would be happy to know someone had captured their son's heart in order to keep it safe. He loved her and he was going to tell her, show her again and again. After all, he had the rest of their immortal lives to let her know how much he loved her.

Every day for the rest of their lives. The bleakness of his immortal life finally lifted with Eirene's arrival.

He turned away from the window and left the room with a smile on his face.

* * * *

"Eirene."

She heard the voice from afar. She heard it again. It was Finn's voice. She opened her eyes immediately, panic gripping her. Finn was calling to her.

"Finn!"

All at once she felt a strong warm band around her waist, pulling her back to the bed. She grabbed the offending restraint as she turned around, and her face hit a muscular wall. She gasped as a hard shaft bumped against her hip. The scent of man and soap assailed her.

She breathed in deeply and looked up to dark midnight blue eyes which crinkled with amusement.

She flung her arms around Finn's neck, raising her mouth to meet his.

"Are you okay?"

"Yes, yes, I'm fine. Thanks to you." Finn cradled her close.

Eirene's need to feel him, taste him and know he was alright overrode everything else. With a groan Finn welcomed her tongue, slanting his mouth to deepen the kiss.

"I missed you so much." Eirene held on to him, helpless yet happy to be tossed in the wave of desire building inside her. She trailed her mouth and tongue against Finn's throat and smiled when Finn hissed as she licked the pulse beating at the base of his neck. She revelled at Finn's callused hands on her body, making her skin quiver underneath his touch.

Finn used his leg to part her thighs before he entered her slowly. He groaned as she accommodated him eagerly. He kissed her, their tongues mating and learning each other. Eirene moaned against Finn's mouth when he thrust deeper. She lifted her legs to encircle his waist, giving him more access. She whimpered when he withdrew, leaving only his cock head inside her to tease her opening.

"Don't do that," she whispered.

"Don't do what?" he asked, chuckling huskily. "How about this?"

Eirene let out a strangled cry when Finn entered again, lifting her up so that his shaft could also tease the sensitive nub in the apex of her nether lips. Liquid heat enveloped Finn in a hot welcome. Her hips lifted at Finn's every thrust, his every sensual push and pull in tandem with his thrusting inside her mouth. Eirene's lips held on to his tongue as she moaned against him. The next time Finn thrust deep, she squeezed her core muscles hard, clamping her velvet sheath around his member. Finn groaned again, burying his head against her neck before his tongue blazed a trail down her neck, past the pulse at the base of her throat, and moving further south to capture a nipple with his mouth. His hand found her other breast and rubbed the other nipple between his thumb and forefinger.

Eirene was in seventh heaven. She rode the gentle crest of their combined desire until Finn began to increase the pace. Her wet sheath contracted every time she heard the slapping of his balls against her tush. She whimpered and gripped his hips, feeling her climax growing inside her. Head thrown back with her eyes closed, Finn's grunts of pleasure lifted her higher. Faster he went. Deeper he thrust. Eirene's cries urged him on, demanding more.

"Yes!" Eirene felt Finn's hard shaft lengthen and thicken inside her. She was becoming delirious with desire. Her body was as taut as a bow string. She reached out for that point of bliss which would allow her to shatter to a million pieces in glorious ecstasy. At last she reached it. Eirene's body jerked with the force of her orgasm. She felt herself scatter. She felt herself drown in rapture. Her channel tightened and with one last thrust, Finn came with a strangled groan, his body trembling as he emptied himself into her.

"I missed you, too," he whispered against her mouth. He was out of breath as if he had run a marathon. He trailed his tongue to lick the shell of her ear and the sensitive skin behind it. She arched her body against Finn as she tingled with pleasure.

"You have such an incredibly sexy way of showing it," she said while caressing his arms.

Finn gave her a lopsided grin before kissing her tenderly. He noticed the marks on her wrist. He caressed the soft skin, then brought it to his mouth to kiss and lick it. Eirene quivered. Slowly the wounds disappeared.

"I'm so glad you're standing up and breathing and...," she said huskily with tears in her voice, breathing in more of his scent. "I didn't want to stay away."

"I know," he said, running his hands down her side, to the dip of her waist and down the side of her thighs. "Zac told me Roarke threatened to ban you from seeing me."

She sighed and nodded before lying on her back, not bothering to cover her breasts with the duvet.

"Why did you go to Dac's club?" he asked, propping his head on his hand.

"I wanted to find Penny," she confessed. "I thought that if Dac had his hands full with the Cynn Cruors, I'd be able to see if I could find clues as to her whereabouts. But I didn't get the chance to do so when all hell broke loose."

"We didn't find any girls either," he stated. "I don't know whether Graeme and the rest found anyone. I was stupid to take my eyes off Dac."

Eirene shifted to curl more into Finn's side. Finn's arm went around her shoulders as he caressed her arm.

"I felt it, you know," she murmured. "I felt the pain you went through." She looked up at him, smiling sadly. "I didn't want you in pain."

"Oh, Eirene," Finn sighed as he gathered her in his arms, holding her tightly against his chest. "You are so selfless. You have brought me back. I want you to always be by my side. You are my strength. I can't believe I have found someone to make my life complete after all this time."

"Well, now that I'm with you, Scatha beware," she said, chuckling.

"Do you always look for danger, babe?" he asked. He smiled in satisfaction at Eirene's moan, and her eyes darkened when he cupped a breast and started playing with her nipple. "Because I'm telling you, by being bonded to me we will be living a life of danger."

"It's not like I court it."

Finn raised a brow.

Eirene sighed, covering his playful hand with hers. "Okay, I guess just a little. But if I wasn't there, you might have died."

Finn lay down and hugged Eirene to his side.

"That was close," he admitted. "Though it's not likely to happen again."

"Why? How?" Eirene rested her chin on his chest, closing her eyes at the delicious shivers running through her as Finn stroked her back.

"As my mate, your blood allows me to heal more quickly than if I wasn't bonded. If I am not bonded, having sex helps quite a bit to regain our strength."

"Oh." Eirene blushed at the memory of their first kiss. Looking at Finn, she realized he remembered it too.

"I need to give you my blood, Eirene."

"I don't understand." She angled her head against the pillow to look at him.

"You need to bite me."

Her eyes widened. "Where?"

"Close to the heart."

"But I don't have fangs like you do."

"When a Cynn Cruor is mated he will need his mate's blood and she will need his. The mate will develop the ability to develop fangs and only for that purpose. Especially, if she is a mortal."

"She? Is there no female Cynn Cruor?"

"None. Unless the Cynn have missed something in our history."

A companionable silence fell around them like a cozy blanket until Eirene's hand drifted down to close around his hard aching shaft before sliding further to gently cup his balls before moving back to shaft again. Finn's jaw clenched in pleasure when Eirene slid her fingers up and down his rod before teasing the slit, laving the fluid that oozed from the tip around his the swollen head. He closed his eyes and just allowed himself to enjoy her touch, making his cock ache to be sheathed inside her satin heat once more.

Eirene straddled him as she continued her stroking. He looked down to see himself harden and lengthen under the spell of her hands. He sighed longingly as she gently twisted the sensitive skin, bringing such delicious friction. A low rumble rippled form his throat as Eirene bent down to lick more of the pre-cum which leaked from him. His heart pounded at seeing her tongue flick around the head while her hands kept their up and down motion.

"Eirene, you keep doing that and I'm going to spill right away."

Her seductive chuckle almost undid him. She rose up to look at him, licking her lips erotically as she positioned her glistening folds above his throbbing rod.

"The only place you'll spill, Finn Qualtrough, is either inside my mouth or inside me."

With one move Eirene took all of him into her. They both sighed in satisfaction. Finn held on to her hips as she threw her head back, showing the column of her throat and the rise and fall of her breasts. Her hair fell softly down her back, while some tendrils fell down to play peek-a-boo with her breasts.

And Finn had never seen such a breathtaking sight.

He watched her through half lidded eyes. His jaw clenched at the effort of stemming the surge of indescribable sexual hunger pouring through every pore of his body, His whole world centred on his shaft so lovingly cosseted by her heat. Low growls erupted from his throat as Eirene unsheathed him only to allow him to plunge headlong up inside of her. She started slow, then increased the tempo. Soft mewls of desire tumbled from her parted lips. His cock savoured the loving caress of her femininity. His hands suddenly gripped the sheets when Eirene rotated her hips, allowing his member to stretch her, but at the same time pamper him as her sex tightened its hold. She leaned forward, dangling her breasts over his face and moaned in delight when he squeezed and pinched her nipples with enough pressure to give her a nip of sweet pain before sucking on them hard. Finn rode on a high. His hips bucked up as he pistoned in and out of her. Every moan and sigh he heard from Eirene magnified his own lust. The woman above him, his mate, drove him wild, making him crave her like a drug.

It was time he took over.

Finn bucked his hips against her mound, causing her to straighten up before one hand gripped her hip and the other pressed hard against her belly as he started to thrust fast.

Eirene screamed his name.

Eirene never felt such intense pleasure as Finn's cock hit her g-spot. That, combined with his pumping hard and fast, threw her over the precipice and she shuddered her orgasm above him. Languor enveloped her body, but Finn's thrusts started the pressure in her sex to coil again, her body burning. Her forehead puckered. The gums around her incisors began to itch. Her heart stuttered as she opened her eyes to look down at Finn. His face was filled with ecstatic bliss. The opalescent glow which surrounded them was breathtaking. It looked like millions of tiny pieces of tinsel glittering around them. Her breath caught in her throat at the swell of emotion inside her. She tentatively flicked the tip of her tongue over her teeth and felt a sharp sting. She had no chance to wonder about how her teeth came to be as a new spiral of arousal slammed into her.

Finn groaned now, holding her hips with both hands as he continued to pound into her.

"Eirene, I'm about to come," he said harshly.

"Oh, God, yes!" she cried out before she fell forward and sank her fangs against the left side of his chest, close to his heart. Dimly she heard Finn roar his orgasm as he called out her name. She felt him shudder underneath her as the warmth of his seed flushed into her core and womb. The coppery taste of blood filled her mouth and heightened her senses. She thought she would gag at its thick texture, but the liquid which coated her mouth was sweet and lightly scented with bergamot. This was Finn's essence in its purest form. The truth brought tears to her eyes. She lovingly suckled against his chest, trying as much as possible not to inflict any pain. But the continuous flow of blood into her mouth made her want more. She held on to Finn's chest while he continued to caress her back. Then she felt her gums slightly open as her blood flowed from her mouth and surged into him. She moaned softly at the pleasure and pain of blood flowing from her while Finn continued to gently move in and out of her. She floated in a sea of unexplainable pleasure as she took her fill while giving in return. She could develop an addiction to his blood, she thought vaguely. It gave her a heady feeling of flying so that she continued to hold on to him lest she fall from some invisible cliff. Finn stopped moving inside her, but she still had so much liquid heat. Tears fell from her closed eyes onto Finn's chest, when she felt him kiss her hair and forehead lovingly.

God, she loved this Cynn Cruor so much, it made her ache inside.

When Eirene drew blood, Finn felt his heart falter before it started beating again as he was cast into a whirlpool of ecstasy. While she suckled, he felt her sweet blood merging with his in his veins. For a moment his blood ran side by side with her blood, then Finn felt his blood fuse with hers. He felt stronger than he'd ever been, his senses sharper than they'd been before. He held her close as she continued to give him her blood. His cock was still hard inside her.

So he lifted his lips slowly. Eirene moaned before her core's muscles squeezed him hard.

With a growl, he shifted so she was lying on her back. Her mouth unlatched from his chest. He saw her cute fangs for a brief moment before they receded and returned to normal. He looked at her eyes. The dark sable pools now had gold flecks in them just like his eyes. Happiness soared through him. He kissed her with urgent tenderness before lapping up the little blood remaining on her mouth and her teeth. Eirene let out a gasp, her body arching when Finn twitched inside her. She looked at him with her gold flecked eyes deep with desire and lifted her legs to rest on the crooks of his arms to give him more access to her sexual heat.

Finn's shaft slowly moved inside her, then withdrew so that only the head was inside her before he thrust in again.

Deep.

In and out, his shaft went. Deep and slow, then hard and fast. Eirene's pants and soft gasps urged him to claim her, to brand her and bind her as close to him as possible. He felt his sacs fill again, the sensation building around his groin area. His heart beat as though he was running a marathon. The faster he thrust, the deeper he went until he could feel the mouth of her womb. Eirene's cries stepped up until she screamed his name again, holding on to his taut hips, and trembling underneath him as the powerful tide of bliss rolled over them. With one last thrust, Finn buried his fangs on her left breast as he too gave more of his blood. He thought he had none left to give, but his head almost exploded when his seed jerked out of his shaft and into Eirene's womb. He let his blood flow into her system as his gums opened. They held on to each other as the afterglow of their lovemaking snugly wound around them. Their heavy breaths mixed with the cool air as their unified hearts slowed down to rest.

    They were now inextricably linked. One couldn't be without the other and if they were apart, their blood would keep them together. Her blood would forever heal her warrior as his blood would forever bind him to her. They would now feel the same pain and loss in the same way they would feel the same passion and bliss.

    They were now Cynn Cruor.

EPILOGUE

It was more than an hour before Finn could leave Eirene's side. He watched her while she slept, exhausted from their lovemaking. He, on the other hand, felt himself getting stronger. His wounds had completely healed as if the gashes had never been there. He marvelled at the woman who was the most beautiful person he had ever seen. Not because of her features, but because of her selflessness, of her desire to help people.

And because he knew without a doubt she loved him as much as he loved her.

Finn made his way to the command centre, wanting the discussion with Roarke over and done with so he could spend the rest of the night with his beloved.

Finn's smile faltered as he entered. Roarke sat on one of the leather armchairs with a glass of scotch in his hand. There was a roaring fire in the fireplace even though it was a balmy night. It was the only light in the room and it cast shadows which danced against the paneled walls and bookshelves. The curtains and windows were wide open to allow cool air to circulate in the room. Finn looked at Roarke, his features harsh with pain.

"Roarke." Finn strode towards his brother. Guilt washed over him. He had been so immersed with Eirene, he had forgotten that he was a Cynn Cruor warrior first and foremost.

"There's nothing to be guilty about Finn," Roarke said as he read Finn's mind, giving him a smile. "I understand your need to be with Eirene."

Finn nodded. He sat down on the armchair opposite Roarke's. He raked his hand through his hair, stealing a glance at his leader. Roarke's face was bleak, his mouth pinched, and his eyes wintry. Damn, what had happened while he was healing?

"Eirene was at the club to find Penny." Finn offered.

Roarke nodded. "Yes. She didn't find Devon's daughter. She told us. Eirene did say there was a hidden room which she was going to investigate. I've asked the other Faestens if they can spare any Cynn mortals to check on the place. Some of the Faestens have mortals as well as warriors working with the police."

"And?"

"Everything is gone," Roarke replied as he massaged his nape tiredly. "As though nothing happened there. I don't know how the people who partied there can believe that club didn't exist. The Cynn Cruors' contacts in the press have kept it out of the news."

Finn nodded. "Anyone who was there will find it difficult to show evidence that Dac's club really existed."

"I agree." Roarke replied. "They found traces of blood close to the hidden door. It's Scatha blood. Probably from the bastard Eirene stabbed. Unfortunately, still no trace of Penny."

While Finn was disappointed that Penny wasn't found, his heart swelled with pride. His mate was such a warrior.

A sexy warrior.

"But that's not what's bothering you. What's happened? Where's Graeme, Blake, Zac?"

Roarke gave him a cursory glance before his mouth lifted in a humourless smile.

"They're fine. Zac's with Devon, checking up on how he's healing before he hits the clubs. After all, it's the night of the full moon."

Finn hadn't forgotten this special night of all nights. A night where he and Eirene could have children. He wasn't able to ask her earlier if she wanted them, but there would always be another full moon.

"And Graeme?" he prodded.

"Graeme has left for the clubs."

"What about Blake?"

"Blake has joined Graeme at Graeme's insistence. After the clubs, Blake is leaving."

"What?" Finn thundered his face incredulous. "Why?"

Roarke rubbed his forehead with his fingers. He shook his head.

"I have no idea why. I asked him, even threatened to report him to the Council of Ieldran, but he didn't balk. He wouldn't tell me or Graeme what was bothering him. He said he had to find out about something. He said it would make or break his being a part of the Cynn Cruors."

"Fuck! I knew Dac has something to do with this. That bastard," Finn swore as he paced in front of the fireplace. He raked his hand through his short hair. "We can't let Dac tear us apart, Roarke. We're stronger than that."

"Yes, we are and I agree with you. Something happened in Dac's club when Blake and Graeme stormed the office. I've asked Graeme what happened but he, too, is as baffled as we are," Roarke said before he knocked back the scotch in his glass. He stood up and went to the bar to pour more of the amber liquid into his glass, filling it almost to the brim. "Our saving grace is that Blake promised he would come back and tell us everything, whether what he finds out frees him of his burden or not."

Finn nodded, but his sharp senses detected something else.

"There's something more. What you've just told me

isn't what's really bothering you," Finn's stated, his eyes narrowed. "Just like with Blake, something happened to you in the club."

Roarke paused from putting the crystal stopper on the decanter's mouth. His mouth pressed into a thin line, letting it pass for a smile.

"You know me so well, Brother."

"I've been saving your arse for hundreds of years, how could I not?" Finn arched a mocking brow.

Roarke chuckled, his face lightening a bit, but he continued to remain silent.

"Well damn it, Mate! What is it?"

Roarke tipped the glass back, drinking all of its contents. His jaw clenched as he wiped his mouth with the back of his hand. He turned to Finn, his eyes dark and haunted.

"I saw someone there, someone I thought I'd never see again."

Finn wore a puzzled frown. "Who?"

"Deanna." Roarke's voice was tight. "She was there. My mate Deanna is alive."

THE END

Thank you for reading Finn and Eirene's story and I hope you liked it. If you are so inclined please leave a review of the book either on Amazon or Goodreads. Reviews help authors made their stories better and help spread the word of their work.

ABOUT THE AUTHOR

I'm just an ordinary woman with a love for reading and baking snickerdoodles and Russian tea cakes. My son loves baking too, well at least after licking the batter off the bowl! I make a mean beef stew derived from my grandmother's secret recipe. Except for my Uncle and me, no one knows exactly how it's done. I love swimming though I don't get to do that much now. Someday, I'd like to go back to it.

I do love myths and legends, love watching documentaries, and I do belong to a huge clan that is scattered across North America, Oceania, and Asia. Now that I'm living in the UK, add Europe.

Another thing that I love? To hear from you. So drop me a message when you can through my contact page and I will definitely reply.

Published by Beau Coup Publishing:
http://www.beaucoupllcpublishing.com/

Visit
Isobelle Cate

Facebook:
https://www.facebook.com/AuthorIsobelleCate
Twitter: https://twitter.com/Isobelle_Cate
Website: http://www.isobellecate.weebly.com/
Amazon Author Page:
http://www.amazon.com/author/isobellecate

More books by Isobelle Cate from Beau Coup Publishing:
Amazon: http://amzn.to/1i833z0

Connect with Isobelle Cate Online:

Isobelle Cate's Facebook Profile and Page:
https://www.facebook.com/AuthorIsobelleCate

Follow Isobelle Cate on Twitter:
https://twitter.com/Isobelle_Cate

Isobelle Cate's Amazon page:
http://www.amazon.com/Isobelle-Cate

Find Isobelle Cate's Books on Goodreads:
https://www/goodreads.com/author/show/7191925.Isobelle_Cate

You can contact Isobelle via email:
isobellecate@gmail.com

Links to Isobelle's books:

Paranormal Romance

The Cynn Cruors Bloodline Series:
Forever at Midnight (Book 2)
http://mybook.to/Forever_at_Midnight

Midnight's Atonement (Book 3)
http://mybook.to/Midnights_Atonement

Midnight's Fate (Book 4)
http://mybook.to/Midnights_Fate

My Haven, My Midnight (Book 5)
http://mybook.to/MyHavenMyMidnight

Contemporary Romance

Second Chances Series
Be Mine (Book 1)
http://mybook.to/Be_Mine

You and I (Book 2)
http://mybook.to/You_and_I_Cate

Standalone

Dying to Live
http://mybook.to/Dying_to_Live

Treagar's Redemption
Amazon: myBook.to/Treagars_amzn
Nook: http://bit.ly/Treagars_Redemption_Nook
Kobo: http://bit.ly/Treagars_Redemption_Kobo
iBooks: http://bit.ly/Treagars_Redemption_iBooks

Historical
Lakam (The Mana Series: Book 1)
http://mybook.to/Lakam

Printed in Great Britain
by Amazon

27093863R00116